FIC   Wersba, Barbara
WER   Fat

$11.25

DATE				
JA 26 '95				
SE 29 '94				
Oct 13 97				

Fat: A Love Story

BARBARA WERSBA

FAT

A LOVE STORY

A CHARLOTTE ZOLOTOW BOOK

HARPER & ROW, PUBLISHERS

The author gratefully acknowledges permission to reprint the following:

From "The Dry Salvages" in FOUR QUARTETS by T.S. Eliot,
copyright 1943 by T.S. Eliot; renewed 1971 by Esme Valerie Eliot.
Reprinted by permission of Harcourt Brace Jovanovich, Inc.

Library of Congress Cataloging-in-Publication Data
Wersba, Barbara.
  Fat, a love story.

  "A Charlotte Zolotow book."
  Summary: During the summer she is sixteen,
overweight Rita Formica falls in love with the most
beautiful young man she's ever seen and is
determined to win him at all costs.
  [1. Weight control—Fiction.   2. Sag Harbor (N.Y.)—
Fiction] I. Title.
PZ7.W473Fat 1987   [Fic]   86-45485
ISBN 0-06-026400-4
ISBN 0-06-026415-2 (lib. bdg.)

Fat: A Love Story

1

THE FIRST THING that was wrong was our names—because my name was Rita Formica, and his name was Robert Swann. These are not names that go together. I mean, can you see the engagement announcement?

> *Mr. and Mrs. Tony Formica*
> *of Sag Harbor, New York, are pleased*
> *to announce the engagement of their daughter Rita*
> *to Robert Swann of East Hampton.*
> *Mr. Swann is a graduate of Choate and Harvard.*
> *Miss Formica is a bicycle messenger.*

I've never seen an engagement announcement, so maybe that's not the form they use. But from the very beginning, I should have known that a person named Rita Formica would have trouble seducing a person named Robert Swann.

I was sixteen years old, working as a bicycle messenger in Sag Harbor, when I met Robert. And if the whole thing hadn't been so funny, it would have been sad, because at that time I was five foot three and weighed two hundred pounds. Not the size of your average speedy bicycle rider. Not the poundage of your average girl athlete.

I had always been fat—a fat baby, a fat child, and now I was a fat teenager. Fat was my fate, so to speak, and like one of those heroes in a Greek play, I couldn't seem to change it. When I was little I had been taken to special doctors and sent away to diet camp, and when I was older I had joined Overeaters Anonymous. But none of it worked. I was a compulsive eater, eating was my life, and I was fat.

My mother, by the way, is a perfect size twelve and very lovely. My father, who owns Tony's Auto Repair on Clarence Street, is also thin. I'm an only child, so this weight problem of mine has always received a lot of attention, but the more they tried to help me—my parents, I mean—the fatter I got. I didn't want help. What I wanted was to eat.

And then I met Robert.

Robert Swann was just like his name—tall, beautiful, upper-class, aristocratic. And thin. He had straw-colored hair that fell over his forehead, and his eyes were the color of blue marbles. There was not an extra ounce of fat on his body, and his muscles rippled like a lion's. He was a health freak, and we met at the Health and Racquet Club in East Hampton.

Sag Harbor, where I live, is part of something on Long Island, New York, that is called the Hamptons— and the Hamptons is probably like no other place in the world. It consists of a lot of little towns strung together near the ocean, and there is a terrific difference here between the rich and the poor. The rich—like Robert Swann—come down for the summer to these big estates by the ocean, and they ride around in Jaguars and Bentleys. They shop at places like The Barefoot Contessa for food, and at Latham House for clothes, and they are always blond and tan, with perfect teeth. If there's anything about rich people that gives them away, it's their teeth. The rest of us—the middle class or the downright poor—go to Stern's or Caldor's for our clothes, and are lucky to drive an old Chevy or Ford. Before I met him, my employer Arnold Bromberg was driving a 1962 Chevy, but it collapsed and we had to conduct Arnold's business by bicycle.

My friend Nicole, who is French, used to say that you can never be too rich or too thin—which is a statement she borrowed from a woman called the Duchess of Windsor. Whenever she would say it, I'd answer, "You're wrong, kid. What you *really* can never be is too poor or too fat." And then we would start to laugh.

5

Back to Arnold Bromberg.

I met Arnold in June, right after school was out, because I answered an ad he had placed in the local paper. As usual, I needed a summer job, and Arnold's ad was interesting. "Deliveryperson wanted," it said, "to deliver pastries for *Arnold's Cheesecake*. No experience necessary." I had never heard of *Arnold's Cheesecake*, but the address was right near my house, which is on Madison Street, so I decided to walk over.

The first thing that seemed odd was that Arnold's place said HARBOR HOUND DOG GROOMING PARLOR outside, and the second thing that seemed odd was that it *was* a dog grooming parlor. A defunct dog grooming parlor with all the fixtures still there. Wire cages for dogs, and bathtubs for dogs, and grooming tables for dogs—and, in the rear of the building, Arnold's cheesecake business. I later learned that the previous tenant, the dog groomer, had skipped town without paying his rent, thus leaving all of his fixtures behind. Arnold didn't know what to do with the fixtures, so he had left them there—living in the back of the store, where there was a combined kitchen and living room.

I stepped into the dog grooming parlor and called, "Hello? Anybody home?" And in two seconds Arnold Bromberg was in the room. He was a huge person with brown curly hair and glasses. I figured that he was around thirty years old.

"I'm answering your ad," I said. "To deliver cheese-cake."

Arnold took off his glasses. "How wonderful," he replied. "I'm delighted to meet you."

I kept watching his face, to see how he would react to my weight, my size, my heft—but he seemed to have no reaction at all. You have no idea how fat people are discriminated against in this world, and how people stare at you the first time they meet you. Arnold didn't stare.

"You're the first person who's answered my ad," he said. "Won't you sit down? My name is Bromberg."

I looked around, but there was no place to sit—so we both leaned against the dog grooming tables. "Cigaret?" said Arnold. I shook my head. "Some iced tea?" he suggested.

"Could you tell me something about this job?" I said. "What does it entail?"

Arnold smiled. "It entails delivering my homemade cheesecake around town, and I would be asking you at this very moment if you have a driver's license, except that my car just died. So I suspect that we'll be delivering the cheesecake by bicycle. Can you ride a bicycle?"

"Well . . ."

"Good," he said, "because we do have a very fine bicycle here, with a basket on the front, and that will have to do for the moment."

"How far would I have to ride? On the bicycle."

7

"I don't exactly know, because my cheesecake business has only been in existence for a month, but it will be mostly the Sag Harbor area. Are you local? Do you live nearby?"

"I live on Madison Street. The white house with the green awning, across from the grocery store."

"Good, good," said Arnold. "Now, would you like to taste the cheesecake? I think it's important that you taste it if you're going to work here."

I followed him into the back of the building, which consisted of a big kitchen–living room, and a sunny bedroom. Both rooms were very neat and lined with books. On a counter in the kitchen were a lot of cheese-cakes. "I'll make us some coffee," said Arnold, "and then we'll have a piece of cake."

I sat down at his kitchen table, wondering what I was getting into. He seemed like a very weird person—though harmless—and I couldn't see myself delivering his cheesecake on a bicycle. "How much do you pay?" I asked. "I have a few other ads to answer."

His face fell—and for a moment I thought he was about to cry. "Other ads? Oh, please don't answer any other ads. I'd *love* you to work here."

Well, of course, that did it. I mean, no one had ever wanted my services that much in my entire life, and I was very impressed. "It's OK," I said. "Don't be upset,

Mr. Bromberg, please. I'll work for you. But I need to know what you pay."

"I'll pay whatever you ask," he said. Which amazed me.

We had a piece of cheesecake together—which was a little on the dry side, I thought—and two cups of coffee, and finally I got up my courage to ask Arnold for five dollars an hour. Which he agreed to. He seemed terrified that I would walk out on him, or change my mind.

"How many cheesecakes do you sell each week?" I asked. "Where do you advertise?"

Arnold finished his coffee and lit a cigaret. "I have ads in all of the local papers. Though I am hoping that word of mouth will do the trick. The cheesecake *is* good, isn't it?"

"Yeah, it really is," I lied.

"When the business gets going, we could do some catering."

"With just cheesecake?"

"No, no, of course not. But I'm rather a good cook, and perhaps the cheesecake will lead to bigger and better things."

I thought he was pretty optimistic, considering how dry the cheesecake was, but I didn't want to discourage him. "Catering is a good business," I said, "here in the Hamptons. So many parties."

He blew a stream of smoke over my head and gazed into the air—as though cheesecakes were passing before his eyes. "If *David's Cookies* is such a success, why not *Arnold's Cheesecake*? Anything is possible."

"It's true."

"All a person needs is faith in himself. Don't you agree?"

"Sure," I said.

He smiled—the smile of a nine-year-old boy. "Then you'll work for me? You'll deliver the cheesecake?"

"Absolutely. When do I start?"

"Tomorrow. At noon. May I ask your name?"

"Rita Formica," I said, hating the sound of it, as always.

"What a beautiful name," said Arnold Bromberg. "So musical."

It was only on the way home that I realized that my mother would have a fit, an absolute fit, when I told her that I was working for a cheesecake company. I had once worked in an ice cream parlor and gained ten pounds. "But sweetie," my mother had said, "it's crazy. How can a person with an eating problem work in an ice cream store?"

"It soothes me to be around ice cream," I had answered. "I don't have to eat it. I just like to be near it."

My mother sighed. "I don't know what to do about you, honey. Your logic defeats me."

It defeated me too, of course, but I didn't want to tell her that. Anyway, I didn't really like cheesecake unless it had strawberries on top, and Arnold's cheesecake wasn't too good in the first place. Strawberries were my passion in those days—strawberry ice cream, strawberry short-cake, strawberry tarts, strawberry Twizzlers. . . . "Arnold Bromberg," I said aloud, as I walked home that day, "you're really odd."

2

BEFORE I GET ONTO the topic of Robert Swann, I have to explain a few things about my eating, my weight, and my personality. The story of me and Robert won't make any sense to you unless you realize what I looked like in comparison to what *he* looked like—and the difference between our backgrounds.

To begin with, I was one of those fat people you often see on the street and feel sorry for. The kind of girl who wears a dress that looks like a tent and who is always munching something out of a bag. The various diet doctors I used to go to would ask me what times of the day I ate, but I could never answer this question—because I ate around the clock. I even woke up once in the middle of the night to discover myself eating while asleep. A Hershey bar with almonds. Sugar was my downfall, though I also binged on bread and potatoes, and to confront me with ice cream was like slipping an alcoholic one drink. I could go through an entire Sara Lee cake in about five minutes. I could eat six candy bars at a time.

What was wrong with me? Was it psychological or physical? Did I have low blood sugar or was I neurotic? Did I have too many fat cells, was my metabolism too slow, had I been orally fixated as a baby? All my life people had been trying to help me answer those questions, trying to help me in general—and all my life I had rebelled against being helped.

Why? Because I liked being fat.

Well, not really. I mean, that's a terrible oversimplification—because most of the time I suffered from being so grotesque. To be fat is a signal to other people that you have no control, no pride, and this is the message that they get about you right away. But it was like I was two people. The first person went to doctors and counselors, and weight camps and therapy groups—and was perpetually on a diet. But the second person, the *real* me, wanted only one thing. To sabotage myself. To eat candy while I was dieting. To walk when I should jog. To skip my meetings of Overeaters Anonymous.

To hide Sara Lee cakes in the bottom of my closet, behind the shoes.

You are familiar, I suppose, with that old cliché that fat people are jolly? Well, it's true. They are jolly as a means of avoiding suicide, and I was no exception. The life of every party, the clown of every group, always popular, always liked—but never loved. Because nobody loves a fat girl. They try to make out with her because she seems like an easy mark, but nobody loves her. And, unlike the people in my class at Peterson High, I was not after round-the-clock sex. Being on the Pill was not exactly my preoccupation.

I suppose I should bring my parents back into the story here, because they are so painfully nice. I say painfully, because to this very day they make me feel guilty about everything. My parents are two of the nicest people in the world, who love each other, who love me, who love our dog Mortimer—and who have tried to help me get thin from the time I was five years old. We are not rich people, but they have spent thousands and thousands of dollars on me. Trying to make me thin. Trying to make me beautiful. Planning for my future. Wanting the best for me. Telling me how much they care. God! Can you imagine the kind of guilt that attitude causes? Sometimes I didn't know which was my main problem—guilt or fat.

My father is a brilliant mechanic, a kind of genius with cars. And deep down he is a sensitive person. But he has a habit of saying things like, "What's up, doc?" or "See you later, alligator" that drives me crazy. He didn't finish high school, whereas my mom, who has a real estate license and works for Apple Realty, had two years of college. We're not wealthy, but we live in a nice house and have a pretty garden in the back. My father is a lapsed Catholic and my mother is Episcopalian. As for me, until quite recently I was an atheist.

Which brings us to that beautiful WASP Robert Swann. And in case you are not familiar with the word WASP, it means White Anglo-Saxon Protestant. In Robert's case, it also means rich, gifted, charismatic, sexy, and thin.

Robert Swann was a graduate of Harvard, and—the summer I met him—was twenty-one years old. He was just out of college and was going to join his father's brokerage firm in the fall. In the winters he lived on Fifth Avenue and 85th Street, in New York City. In the summers he lived on Cobblers' Lane, in East Hampton. This was his last summer of freedom before going to work for his father—and so Robert was determined to make the most of it, determined to go to the beach every day, and play tennis, and get a tan, and—most of all— to work out at "the club," which is what everyone calls the Health and Racquet Club. Fitness is a very big deal in the Hamptons. Especially for the rich. I mean, it is not unusual to see people in their workout clothes at cocktail parties, and almost everyone on the street during the summers is either jogging, or just finishing jogging, or just about to jog. Why Robert Swann had such a thing about fitness, I will never know, because he was *already* fit, already gorgeous, but fitness and good health were his thing. He did not drink or smoke, and did not do drugs. But he did make love. A lot. That part of the story, however, comes later.

As for me, I had only known two realities in my life—compulsive eating and compulsive dieting. The thing that baffled me was that I was hungry twenty-four hours a day. Other people seemed to get hungry at mealtimes. *I* got hungry every five minutes. When I walked through the town of Sag Harbor, it was like a soldier walking through a minefield. Food was everywhere. In bakery stores and supermarkets. In the deli, where they sold homemade donuts, and in the dime store, where they had amazingly good Gummy Bears. Food was lurking in Hildegarde's Tea Shop, where they made pecan pie, and in the Heavenly Cafe, where the cheeseburgers were the best in the world. There were days when the town of Sag Harbor seemed to be constructed of nothing but food, and there was no way to escape it.

Not true. The way to escape it was through not eating at all. I don't mean dieting, and I don't mean medically

15

supervised fasting. I just mean Not Eating. And this is something I did regularly—because it was the only relief I had from the pull, the allure, the seductiveness of food. But then, after around two days of Not Eating, I would faint. So that wasn't the best solution. The thing that I never understood about my eating was that I didn't really enjoy the food in the first place.

Then there was the way I ate at home—which my father described as a kind of vacuum cleaner going through the house, sucking up anything edible. And finally, there were my clothes. Like most fat females, I didn't feel that I deserved to have nice clothes, and so I wore some very peculiar outfits. Huge shapeless sweaters, overalls, raincoats. Boots. Nicole used to say I looked like a fat spy—which I accepted from her because she was my friend. But in a way she was right. I looked like an overweight spy slinking through the streets of London or Berlin. I also wore berets in winter, and visored caps in summer, that I bought at the Army-Navy store.

Robert Swann, of course, looked like he had just stepped out of *Esquire* magazine. The most expensive kind of workout clothes during the day. Beautiful sportswear at night. White chinos, madras shirts, a heavy gold I.D. bracelet on one wrist, a navy cashmere sweater around his shoulders. In my mind's eye I see Robert as being all blond and navy and white. I see him as being made of eighteen-carat gold and white bucks and socks that were always clean. I see his hair as being perpetually scrubbed with Vidal Sassoon shampoo.

And his car! It is not easy to have a spectacular car in the Hamptons, where all the cars—the rich people's, I mean—are spectacular, and waxed to the point where they shine like glass. The summer people here drive Jags and Bentleys and Maseratis, but do you know what Robert Swann drove? Something called a Jensen Arrow. I had never even heard of a Jensen Arrow, but of course the minute I saw it, I knew it had to be his car, because it looked just like him—all blond and navy and white. It was a vintage car, but I never knew which vintage. All I can tell you is that it was creamy white, with navy leather seats and a dashboard made of pale wood.

Next, there was his personality, which I found to be smooth and good-natured and suave, and serious and witty and sensitive—all at once. Robert Swann was as smooth and elegant as I was klutzy, and I swear to God he could have been a bigger star in the movies than Robert Redford. People were always telling him that he should have been an actor, but Robert wasn't interested in anything so frivolous. He was going to be a stock-broker like his dad, and make millions to add onto the millions they already had.

If you're thinking that I was after his money, you're wrong. Dead wrong. It wasn't his money I wanted, it was *him*, every beautiful inch of him, his body and his soul. To me, Robert Swann was the epitome of perfection. He was like one of those medieval knights who dedicate themselves to purity. His only failing was that he wanted constant sex.

"Why, to you, is this a character defect?" Nicole asked me, much later on. "Why, to you, is it something soiled? This man, this Robert, is like a fine American race horse. He is *quivering* with sexiness."

Well, if I had been the object of Robert's quivering, it might have been OK. But I wasn't, and that was the part that caused me so much pain. To know that that beautiful body existed and that I could not have it, was like knowing that there was a gallon of Häagen Dazs ice cream somewhere in the world going to waste. Yes, it's true. I equated Robert with ice cream, with food. I wanted to consume him.

About Nicole. She was—and is—three years older than me, and I met her when she went to work at the Heavenly Cafe. As fat and klutzy as I was, Nicole was tiny and thin and petite. The kind of woman who can put on a big oversized T-shirt, belt it in the middle, create a dress, and stride away on a pair of high heels. Nicole is outrageously sexy, and came to Long Island from Paris with her boyfriend George. But the minute they moved here and became residents, they broke up. Which left Nicole stranded in the Hamptons, upon which she became a waitress. Nicole has masses of dark-red hair, which she piles on top of her head, and she is always dressed in some outrageous costume. Like that T-shirt, belted in the middle. It was odd that she should like me, and I her, but the first time she waited on me at the Heavenly we struck up a conversation. I thought her French accent was kind of humorous, and she found me humorous too, in a different way.

"You are really ordering two cheeseburgers and two strawberry malteds?" she asked me that day. "Fantastic."

"I'm hungry," I said. "Starved."

"That is obvious," she replied. "Permit me an introduction. Nicole Sicard."

"I'm Rita Formica," I said. We shook hands.

Forgetting that she was the waitress and I was the customer, Nicole sat down at my table. "I have seen you before," she stated. "I have been curious about you."

I was very flattered. I mean, she was a real beauty and I was simply me—the klutz of Sag Harbor. "Have you worked here long?" I asked.

She tossed back her beautiful head. "Only this week. It is a fantastic experience."

All of a sudden we had a million things to say to each other. There was no introductory period, no tryout time, we were simply friends on the spot. She told me her history, I told her mine, and both of us—for around twenty minutes—forgot about my cheeseburgers. But then the owner of the Heavenly, Mr. Minelli, came over to our table and looked at us rather oddly. So Nicole rushed back to the kitchen and got my food.

From that day on, I ate most of my meals at the Heavenly Cafe. It was amazing that Nicole didn't get fired for spending so much time with me, but we were really attracted to each other, in the sense that opposites attract. We just couldn't stop talking, and on her day off, which was Wednesday, we would take long walks together on the beach. Nicole was nineteen but she could have been forty—that's how much traveling she had done, and that's how many men she had been involved with. Her relationship with George had lasted for a year, and now she was determined to stay single. "I play the field now," she said to me. "I fool around."

My parents, of course, were disturbed that I was eating so many meals away from home—but there wasn't much they could do about it. All through my childhood they had tried to control my food, but overeaters are like junkies. If they want to do their thing, you can't really stop them. "Please, baby," my father would say. "Try to *think* about what you're doing. Try to have some self-control." But that was like suggesting self-control to Attila the Hun. I mean, self-control was not the issue here.

20

When I look back on my life, I do not see a series of events—I see a long trail of food. A long road littered with candy bars, Sara Lee cakes, ice cream sandwiches, pizzas, jelly donuts, and my beloved Gummy Bears. I gaze into the far-off skies and see, not a sunset, but a cloud of cotton candy, a haze of marshmallow. I'm a very different person now—but in those days food was my god and my religion. Until I met Robert.

3

I STARTED WORK AT *Arnold's Cheesecake* the day after my interview with Mr. Bromberg, at twelve o'clock noon. My mother had almost fainted when I had told her that I was going to work for a cheesecake company, but slowly, patiently, I explained to her that I didn't *like* cheesecake—which she remembered was the truth. As far as I was concerned, it was essential that I have a summer job so that I could continue to eat at the Heavenly Cafe. Cheeseburgers and malteds, roast beef platter with gravy and mashed potatoes, pizza, hot-fudge sundaes.

Arnold Bromberg was waiting for me that day, a

white apron on over his clothes, his curly hair slicked back. He had been making cheesecakes. "Where do I begin?" I asked him. "What do I do?"

He stared at me. "How lovely you look today, Miss Formica. If I may say so."

Lovely? I was wearing a pair of blue overalls and one of my father's shirts. A straw hat. Jogging shoes. As a tribute to my first day's work I had put on lipstick, but crookedly.

"Uh, thank you, Mr. Bromberg," I said. "You look nice too."

"Isn't it glorious outside? Such enormous clouds."

I glanced out the front door of the dog grooming parlor, and saw that there were indeed big fluffy clouds drifting over the harbor. "Yeah," I said, "it's a pleasant day. Have you got some orders for me to deliver?"

Arnold looked sheepish. "Well, not really. Not at the moment. But there are a million things you could help me with, if you don't mind."

"Like what?"

He scratched his head. "Well . . . like going to the post office for me, and picking up some coffee at the grocery store. You could also take a spin on the bicycle and see if it suits you. It's a man's bike, I'm afraid."

My heart sank when he said that, because I wasn't too steady on a woman's bike, much less a man's. But what the hell, I thought. The guy is paying me five dollars an hour. I should try to cooperate.

I did his errands for him in town, and then I rode up and down the block on his bicycle. It wasn't in very good shape, but it did have a roomy basket. I wondered, however, how I would keep the cheesecakes from getting shaken up as I traveled from place to place.

"You don't want me to do any deliveries?" I asked again, when I had put his bicycle in the yard.

Arnold sat down with me on the back porch and lit a cigaret. "Actually," he confessed, "business is a bit slow at the moment, so there isn't anything to deliver. Would you like a piece of cheesecake with some coffee?"

I didn't want to hurt his feelings, so I said sure, of course. And in a few moments he had brought an entire cheesecake and two mugs of coffee out to the porch. I wondered if I would have to eat cheesecake for the duration of my job with him. I wondered if it would make me sick.

We ate the cheesecake, and drank the coffee, and then Arnold lit another cigaret. "Have you always lived in the Hamptons?" he asked.

"Yeah," I said, "I was born here. At Hampton Hospital."

"I'm from Kansas. Topeka, to be exact."

"No kidding? What brought you to Sag Harbor?"

Arnold Bromberg stared into space. "The name," he said, "the romance of the name."

"I beg your pardon?"

"I thought the name was beautiful, and the idea of living on a *harbor* seemed wonderful to me. I mean, Kansas has very few harbors."

"Are you glad you came?"

Mr. Bromberg gave me his little boy's smile. "I have never regretted a single thing in my life, Miss Formica. My life seems wonderful to me."

I had never heard anyone say that before. I mean, most people will tell you that their lives stink, that nothing is going right for them, and that if they only had more money or more sex, or a better house or a better wife, that *then* they could be happy. So I was impressed with Arnold Bromberg's attitude. "Tell me more," I said. Which he proceeded to do.

Arnold Bromberg, it turned out, was a minister's son who had always had a big thing about the ocean and boats, and shorebirds and hurricanes. He had spent his entire life reading about these things, and he would put all these maps of the Atlantic Seaboard on the wall of his room. One day he had bought a map of Long Island to put up on his wall, in Kansas, and upon reading this map he had discovered the Hamptons. Southampton, East Hampton, Bridgehampton, Water Mill, Wainscott, etc. But it was the words "Sag Harbor" that overwhelmed him—so much so that he had packed up his things and moved here. All of which struck me as funny, because Sag Harbor is referred to by some people as "the tacky Hampton." This was a factory town in the nineteenth century, and still looks a bit seedy despite all the restaurants and antique shops. The really rich people live in the other Hamptons. The oddballs and eccentrics live here.

As Arnold continued his story, I began to wonder first about his sanity, and second about his solvency. Because, in the fourteen months he had lived in Sag Harbor, he had run three businesses. The first was called *The Pampered Plant*, which was supposed to be plant care in your home—and when that had gone bust he had invented a service called *The Electric Minstrel*, which consisted of Arnold with an electric guitar, playing at evening parties. When that one hadn't brought in any customers, he had purchased a flock of goats, thinking that he could rent them out and save people the trouble of mowing their lawns. Now he had arrived at *Arnold's Cheesecake*, which, something told me, was not going to fare much better.

"What did you call the goat business?" I asked him.

"*Hampton Rent-a-Goat*. It's a good name, don't you think?"

"Well . . . "

"The difficult part was getting rid of the goats when the business failed," said Arnold Bromberg. "I had gotten so fond of them."

25

All of a sudden I wanted to tell him how dry his cheesecake was—thus preventing another business failure—but somehow I couldn't. He was such a trusting person and so totally optimistic. I bet that no one had told him the truth in his entire life.

"I did keep one goat," Arnold was saying, "named Daisy. I'm boarding her on a farm in Wainscott."

"No kidding. Can't you keep her here?"

Arnold smiled sadly. "The yard is too small, I'm afraid. But I do visit her every Sunday. Perhaps one Sunday you'd like to come along."

"Of course," I said, "of course." But privately I was thinking that either Arnold Bromberg was crazy, or he was what Nicole calls *un original*, which means someone very odd and rare.

I glanced at my watch and realized that I had been with Arnold for two hours. "I guess I should be going," I said. "Unless you have something else for me to do."

His face fell. "Must you leave? I've enjoyed your company so much."

"Well, thank you, Mr. Bromberg. But I really should get along now."

He reached into his back pocket, took out a checkbook, and began to write a check. "Your salary," he explained.

"You don't have to pay me for today, Mr. Bromberg. Really. I mean, I didn't *do* anything."

Arnold Bromberg gazed at me. His eyes, I realized, were sea green. "You did a great deal," he said. "But most of all, you lent your lovely presence to my home. And you shared your thoughts with me. And I am grateful."

I took the check for ten dollars from him, feeling like I was taking candy from a baby. I wasn't a financial wizard, but even I could see that Arnold was going to go broke if he continued to pay me for doing nothing. "Why don't you lower my salary?" I suggested. "Until the business is on firmer ground."

Arnold looked shocked. "I wouldn't hear of such a thing. Five dollars an hour was our agreement."

"But your cheesecakes only cost ten dollars apiece. And if you pay me five dollars an hour . . ."

"My dear Miss Formica, you mustn't worry about this. Leave the business matters to me."

"Well, OK, if that's how you want it."

"It is. Truly."

"Well then, good-bye, Mr. Bromberg."

"See you on the morrow," he said. Which should have sounded silly, but didn't. At least, not with him saying it. There was definitely something Shakespearean about Arnold Bromberg, I decided as we shook hands. "Have a good day," I said.

"I will," he replied, "I know I will. And I hope that you have a good day, too."

"Right," I said. "Absolutely." And then I escaped.

Nicole's phrase suited this guy, I thought as I strolled home that afternoon. He was definitely odd. *Un original.*

4

I AM NOW READY to take the plunge and tell you about Robert Swann. It has taken me all these pages, all these words, to be able to do this. Why? Because to this day, the thought of Robert Swann causes me pain. Not that I'm still in love with him—not at all—but because I made such a horse's ass of myself that summer.

I first saw Robert on June 10th, at four in the afternoon, on the corner of Carriage Lane in East Hampton. He was going into the Health and Racquet Club, and I was going into the dry cleaner's next door. My mother and I were in East Hampton that day doing errands because sometimes we prefer to shop there rather than Sag Harbor. There's a bookstore in East Hampton, and a good dry cleaner's, and a photo store where Mom gets stuff for her camera.

Anyway, she had gone off to The Barefoot Contessa, to get some special kind of vinegar for her salad dressing, and I was carrying a load of stuff into the cleaner's when

I spotted Robert. He was sauntering down the street in very short navy shorts, and a white T-shirt, and white jogging shoes. Even though it was early in the season he had a good tan, and his hair was the color of corn silk in the sun. He was carrying a canvas bag, also navy, and from where I stood I could see the color of his eyes. Bright blue, hard blue. The color of marbles.

I watched him enter the club, and then—to the amazement of the dry cleaning man—I dropped all the stuff I was carrying and followed after Robert. It was like he was the Pied Piper and I was one of those children who get led away. I simply left my mother's dry cleaning on the floor of the shop and drifted after Robert into the club. It was like I was hypnotized. But at the same time I was also highly awake, and highly conscious that something monumental had happened to me. Because, I swear to you, all I had to do was look at Robert Swann for ten seconds to know that I was in love with him. People speak of love at first sight—but that's not what this was. This was love at first glimpse. Ten seconds' worth. Amazing.

I followed him into this very strange environment, with electronic music being played in the background, and down a flight of carpeted steps into a big room that startled me. Because the room was filled with exercise machines called the Nautilus. All kinds of people were working out on these machines, some of them very scantily clad, and because the room was mirrored it gave the impression that the people went on and on into the distance.

It was like I had stepped into the twenty-first century—that's how weird the whole thing seemed to me. Robert Swann walked up to the desk, signed in, and grinned at the girl who was sitting there. "Hi, sweetie," he said. "Hi, babe," she said back.

So. I had heard his voice. And of course it was beautiful. Masculine but sensitive. Cultured without being snobbish. He disappeared into the men's locker room.

I went up to the desk and said hello to the girl, suddenly aware of how fat I must look to her, how grotesque. She was around a size six or something. Blond. Wearing a leotard. "How much does it cost to join this club?" I asked.

She handed me a price sheet. "We're on special this month. It's a real bargain."

Bargain? One month at the club cost a hundred dollars. Three months cost two hundred and seventy-five. I had just received five hundred dollars for my sixteenth birthday, so I made a quick decision. "I'll sign up for three months. But I don't have a checkbook with me or anything."

"That's all right," said the girl. "Just leave a small deposit."

I fished around in the pocket of my overalls and found

five dollars. "Would five dollars be enough?"

"Sure. What's your name?"

In the second that it took her to say, "What's your name?" I decided to invent a new name for myself. "Skylar Cunningham," I said. "From Southampton."

The girl didn't blink an eye. "I'll enroll you starting today."

Skylar Cunningham, I said silently. Skylar Cunningham. It was the beginning of the New Me.

At that moment, Robert Swann came out of the locker room and headed for the Nautilus machines. The one he chose was the one where you sit down and move your torso from side to side, holding on to a bar that provides resistance. I looked at Robert's face and saw that he was totally absorbed in what he was doing, totally absorbed in his torso. "What's that man's name?" I said to the girl at the desk.

"Robert Swann," she said, "and my name's Betsy. Here's your club kit."

She handed me a packet of material about the Health and Racquet Club, but my eyes were still on Robert. "Where does he live?" I asked.

She shrugged. "I don't know. Here in town somewhere."

"Do you spell his name with one *n* or two?"

Betsy was looking at me a little oddly. "Two."

"Do you know how old he is?"

She laughed. "Are you an investigator or something?"

I glared at her. "How could I be an investigator?"

"I don't know. I mean, you ask so many questions."

"I'm a writer," I said, "a novelist. Curiosity is part of my job."

"Gee, no kidding. You look awfully young to be a writer."

"Well, I am one nevertheless. I've been publishing for years."

I could tell that she didn't know whether to believe me or not. "Would you like the grand tour?" she asked. "Of the club, I mean."

"Sure. Lead the way."

By now, of course, I knew that Betsy was regarding me with a certain amount of pity, because of my size. And the more she led me around the club, the more self-conscious I became. Because everyone was thin. Why are all these people here? I wondered. Every one of them is beautiful.

Feeling like an elephant in a field of gazelles, I allowed Betsy to guide me past tanning rooms and massage rooms, into an aerobics room and through a room with stationary bicycles in it. There was a snack bar where one bought fruit juices and Perrier, and two racquetball courts. There was a very glamorous swimming pool. There was also a meditation corner—surrounded, I might add, by potted palms.

"We have all kinds of activities here," Betsy told me. "I think you'll like it."

I decided to take the plunge. "Do any fat people come to this club?"

She didn't blink an eye. "Sure, of course. We have a diet counselor. She's included in the price of admission."

"No kidding. What method does she use?"

"She's eclectic. But she really gets results. Try her."

Alas. By the time we had returned to the Nautilus room, Robert Swann was gone. Where had he vanished to? The tanning room, the meditation corner? Was he at this very moment in the pool, swimming like a champion? "What are your hours here?" I asked Betsy. "Eight in the morning till nine at night," she replied. "We try to accommodate."

Suddenly I remembered my mother's dry cleaning— and also my mother, who was probably at this very moment wandering up and down the streets of East Hampton looking for me. "I have to go," I said. "Thank you for everything. See you tomorrow."

"Come in workout clothes!" Betsy called as I headed up the staircase. "Bring a leotard!"

As I stepped out into the sunlight, I realized to my amazement that nothing had changed. East Hampton was going on just as it had before, cars whizzing by, dogs strolling up the street, people eating ice cream cones. The summer world was the same, but I had changed. I ran into the dry cleaning store.

The clothes were still there, lying in a heap on the floor. Through the plate glass window I could see my mother coming up the street from The Barefoot Contessa. I felt that I had been away for five hours, but it was more like fifteen minutes.

"Skylar Cunningham," I said aloud. "Skylar as in skylark."

And for just one moment I saw myself thin. I mean, really thin and totally beautiful. It was the first time in my life that that had ever happened.

5

NICOLE WAS STANDING by my table in the Heavenly Cafe, ready to take my order. "I'll have a garden salad," I said, "and a very small Diet Coke."

"What is this?" said Nicole. "Some kind of crazy joke?"

"No," I said, "it isn't. I'm dieting."

She put her pad and pencil away and sat down at the table with me. "But my darling mouse, you are *always* on the diet. And it never work."

"It'll work this time," I declared. "I'm in love."

Her eyes widened. "Fantastic! When does it happen? Who is the man?"

I hesitated for a moment, not certain whether I should tell her or not. I mean, Nicole and I were bosom friends, but I had only seen Robert yesterday for the first time and my emotions were raw. I could have burst into tears at the slightest provocation. I felt as vulnerable as a kitten.

"I can't talk about it yet," I said. "It's too new."

Nicole glanced around to see if Mr. Minelli was watching. Surreptitiously, she lit a cigaret. "My darling, I understand. It was the same way when I meet Norman. I feel all damp and crushed, like a rose petal."

"Exactly," I said.

"When I meet Norman, I feel like a wounded butterfly, something very small and frail."

A pause here to explain that Norman was Nicole's new boyfriend. I had met him only the other day and had been very disappointed because, first of all, Norman was short and stocky, and second of all because he was planning to be a bullfighter—a sport I disapproved of. I also wondered how Norman was going to become a bullfighter in Brooklyn, which is where he lived. I was distressed about Norman in general because I didn't think he was good enough for Nicole. She, however, seemed to be mad about him. "He makes the love most beautifully," she had said. "In the sack, he is a little Mozart."

As Nicole went back to the kitchen to place my order, I thought about my own amorous background—which was nil. What I mean is, I was a virgin and had begun to suspect that that status would remain unchanged for the rest of my life. It wasn't that people didn't want to make out with me. They always did. But only because I was fat and therefore—as I told you earlier—seemed like an easy mark. From the eighth grade onward boys had been trying to get me alone in closets, in the backseats of cars, and in the bottom of empty swimming pools. But the whole thing filled me with disgust, if you want to know the truth, because I knew none of them loved me. And it was love I was after. Love with someone extraordinary, like Robert Swann.

It wasn't just that he was gorgeous. It was that I had seen something *underneath* the good looks, something sensitive and wonderful that promised a fantastic future. Behind that beautiful face and those hard blue eyes lurked a poet maybe, or some kind of artist. In addition to which, I felt that we had known each other before. I once had a history teacher named Mrs. Orshinsky, who would tell us that she believed we had all lived other lives, and that was why we sometimes connected with strangers. It was an interesting idea, and it explained my violent feelings for Robert Swann. Who would Robert have been, in some other life? Chopin. And I—with a stretch of the imagination—might have been his lover

George Sand, that terrific woman who dressed in trousers and smoked cigars and didn't give a good goddam what anyone thought.

Nicole returned to my table—with the salad and the Diet Coke—and then she hurried away to wait on other people. Every so often she would pass my table and give me a little wink, as though to say, "Darling mouse, we will talk further!" but my thoughts were gone again. In fact, I was so busy thinking that I didn't even taste the salad. It was diet food and I was eating it—period. What I had to figure out now was how I was going to meet Robert Swann. The health club would serve two purposes—first to make me thin, and second to let me brush shoulders with Robert every day. Because I was sure he went there every day, to work out, to swim, to make himself even more perfect than he was. Would I ever have the courage to speak to him? Not as Rita Formica. But Skylar Cunningham was another matter.

I had eaten the salad without suffering. I had drunk the Diet Coke. And now I was paying my check and waving good-bye to Nicole. She gave me a look that meant, "Are you going already?" and I pantomimed back that I would call her that night. I needed to be alone, to plan the rest of my life, and as I stepped out onto the sidewalk everyone in Sag Harbor looked thin. There were days when everyone on the street looked fat to me, and days when everyone looked unbelievably slender. This was a Slender Day. Girls with the tiniest hips in the world were passing by with their boyfriends. Skinny matrons were going into the grocery store. Even the town dogs, who always patrol the streets of Sag Harbor, looked lean and purposeful. Me too, I thought, as I silently greeted everyone. Me too.

I ARRIVED AT *Arnold's Cheesecake* that day to find Arnold Bromberg waiting for me on the front steps. He was immaculately groomed, as usual, and seemed very excited. "Miss Formica!" he said. "Come inside. Something wonderful has happened."

I followed him into the dog grooming parlor wondering what could have taken place since yesterday. I had left him at two o'clock and seen Robert on the streets of East Hampton at four. "Sit down," he said, "oh, do sit down. I have something to tell you."

I couldn't find anything to sit down *on*, so we stood facing each other. "We have received an order," said Arnold Bromberg, "from a woman in North Haven. She wants two cheesecakes for a dinner party she is giving tonight. She saw our ad in the paper."

"Oh," I said. "Well. That's very nice, Mr. Bromberg."

"Nice? It is more than nice, Miss Formica, it is the beginning of our future. I *knew* the business would catch hold if we could just be patient. And now things are humming."

I didn't see how an order for two cheesecakes could constitute a major breakthrough, but I didn't want to dampen his spirits. I smiled encouragingly.

"Her name is Mrs. Nixon," said Arnold. "No relationship to the ex-president, thank goodness, and a very nice-sounding woman. I said that our messenger would be delivering the cakes at once. I am really very encouraged."

"Well," I said.

Arnold leaned against one of the dog grooming tables. "We must place ads in other newspapers. We must expand."

"Actually . . ."

"In fact, I am thinking of renting a small airplane to fly over Sag Harbor with a banner behind it, advertising our product. The banner might say, CHEERS FOR CHEESECAKE, or perhaps ALL THE WAY WITH ARNOLD'S."

"Wouldn't that be expensive?"

"I don't know," said Arnold happily. "I just know

that we are about to take off. If *David's Cookies* is making millions, we can too. All we need is courage and perseverance."

I had only had one boiled egg for breakfast, and then the garden salad at the Heavenly—and I was feeling a little faint. "Could I have a cup of coffee before I leave?" I asked. "North Haven's a long ride."

"Of course, my dear, of course," said Arnold Bromberg. "Come back to the kitchen with me."

"How lovely you look today," he said, as he put the coffeepot on the stove. "So fresh and winning."

I blushed. Because, secretly, I had hoped that I did look a little better than usual. I was wearing a black leotard and black tights—purchased that morning at Shirlee's Dress Shop—and over the whole outfit I had put on a pale pink mumu, a tentlike affair that my mother had made for me last month. I wondered what it would be like to bike to North Haven in a mumu. Damn. I hadn't thought of that.

"Here are the cheesecakes," said Arnold, when I had finished my coffee. "They are very well boxed and should survive the trip safely. The address is Grove Street, just before the ferry."

I did some quick mental arithmetic. Grove Street was at least three miles away.

"Now," said Arnold, as though he were briefing his

troops, "I have placed a small umbrella in the bike basket, in case it rains, and there is a thermos of springwater
there too, in case you should grow thirsty. If you have
any difficulty you may phone me, but I suspect that
everything will go as planned."

I wanted to salute him, so military did he seem at that
moment, so utterly confident. We walked out to the
back yard, where the bicycle was waiting, and Arnold
fitted the cheesecakes into the bike basket. "If they wish
to pay by check, that is acceptable," he said. "Though
cash, of course, is always better."

"Right. Well, so long now."

"One more thing," said Arnold Bromberg. "You may
tell Mrs. Nixon that we will soon be doing some catering, and that she might want to avail herself of our
services. I suspect that she entertains a great deal."

"What makes you think that?" I asked, trying to bal-
ance on the bicycle.

"The voice," said Arnold, "the voice on the phone.
It was so utterly charming."

I was already on my way down the drive, wobbling
a little, and trying to keep the cheesecakes from sliding
around in the bike basket. "Good-bye, Miss Formica,
good-bye!" called Arnold. "Good luck!"

I pedaled out to Bay Street, and from there onto the
North Haven bridge. I was sweating profusely and was

quite worried that my pink mumu would get tangled in the wheels. I hitched it up around my hips, keeping one eye on the cheesecakes and the other eye on the road. Behind me, a car horn blared. "Watch where you're going, fatty!" someone yelled.

My heart sank, but I kept on pedaling. Over the bridge and along Route 114. By now I was really worried about the cheesecakes, because they were sliding around in the bike basket like mad. What would they look like when Mrs. Nixon opened the boxes?

It took me forty minutes, but finally I arrived at Grove Street. I turned right, and in front of a large frame house was a sign that said, "Nixon." I parked my bike, retrieved the cakes, and went up on the porch and rang the bell. I was exhausted.

Mrs. Nixon opened the door, and it only took me one second to see that Arnold had been wrong. She was not charming. She was, in fact, a very mean broad who looked annoyed about everything. "Are you the messenger?" she said. "Are those the cheesecakes?"

"Yes, ma'am," I replied. "*Arnold's Cheesecake.* At your service."

She took the boxes from me, sat down on a porch chair, and opened one of the lids. She peered into the box, and unable to contain myself, I peered too. The form inside was no longer recognizable as a cake. It looked more like a pudding.

"You could push it back together," I said. "It's just a little out of shape."

The woman glared at me and opened the second box. The cheesecake inside was, if anything, in worse condition than the first. "This is what I'm paying twenty dollars for?" she asked.

It was obviously a rhetorical question, because she didn't let me reply. "This is what I had to go and order for my dinner party?" she asked. "This mess?"

"The cakes can be reconstructed," I said firmly. "They can be fixed."

The woman rose to her feet and handed the boxes back to me. "I'm not paying for this crap," she said. "What are you people? Communists?" She went inside, slamming the door behind her.

I bicycled back to town with an empty feeling in my stomach—half hunger, and half despair. How could I tell Arnold Bromberg that his cheesecakes had been turned down? A person like Arnold could commit suicide over such news. I had a vision of him jumping into the harbor with all his cheesecakes.

Suddenly I realized that I wouldn't tell him at all. At the corner of Clarke Street, I ditched the two cakes in a trash can and took twenty dollars out of my purse. I would not be responsible for Arnold's demise.

He was waiting for me as I pedaled up to the dog grooming parlor—standing on the porch with an eager expression on his face. "Did it go well?" he asked breathlessly. "Was Mrs. Nixon pleased?"

I debarked from the bicycle and sat down, a little heavily, on the front steps. "Yeah," I said, "it went fine. Here's the twenty bucks."

"But did she really like the cakes?"

"She *liked* them," I declared. "Believe me, she liked them."

Arnold took the money from me as though it were the Holy Grail. "Success," he said, "is only a matter of faith. If one believes in success, it will come to him. The universe is benevolent."

The universe may be benevolent, I wanted to reply, but if this situation continues I'm going to be bankrupt.

"Would you like to come inside and rest?" asked Arnold gently. "Would you like a piece of cheesecake?"

I knew that if I had to contemplate any more cheesecake I would throw up. In fact, I was closer to throwing up than I had realized. So—after learning that there were no more orders that day—I bid Arnold good-bye and took off. My mother was going to drive me to East Hampton for my first day's workout at the club. Thrilled that I had joined such an organization, she had packed a little bag for me with gym clothes and a bathing suit in it.

But as we drove over to the club that day, I was less than thrilled myself. For the first time, I wondered what on earth I had done. Most of all, I wondered how I would ever bring myself to speak to Robert Swann.

7

I DIDN'T. At least, not the first day. That first day at the club was a kind of nightmare, with good old Betsy trying to show me the ropes, and me resisting completely. I couldn't learn how to work the Nautilus machines, and the aerobics class was so intimidating that I simply stood in the rear of the room and watched. I didn't want to have a massage because you have to be *naked* to have a massage, and the minute Betsy guided me to the pool I knew I would never get into it. To get into the pool I would have to wear a bathing suit, and there is no one in a bathing suit who looks quite as fat as me. Also, my second day of dieting was making me feel faint. Images of squashed cheesecakes kept passing before my eyes, mingled with the sad spectacle of Arnold Bromberg, thrilled over his newfound success. Also, I couldn't seem to connect with Robert. When I was in the aerobics class, he was in the pool, and when I stood by the pool, he had gone to the Nautilus. I saw him, but we kept passing like ships in the night. Once again he was wearing his tiny navy shorts and a white T-shirt. Once again he looked like a Greek god.

"What time does that person, Mr. Swann, come here each day?" I said to Betsy. "Three o'clock? Four?"

"Four, I think," she replied, giving me one of her looks. "If you're not going into the pool, how about the sauna?"

"What do you wear in a sauna?"

"Nothing. A towel."

So I skipped the sauna, and the pool, and everything else—and after a while, Betsy gave up on me and went back to the desk. I had already been at the club for an hour and a half, and had accomplished nothing. Pretty soon, my mother would be coming to get me. And then I saw Robert Swann getting ready to leave.

He emerged from the men's locker room with his navy canvas bag and bounded up the stairs. Without thinking, I raced into the women's locker room, got my stuff, and followed close on his heels. Betsy was watching all this suspiciously, but I didn't care. I had to see where Robert was going, and if he was going by foot or by car.

As luck would have it, it was by car. His beautiful white Jensen Arrow with the navy leather seats was parked at the curb. He threw his canvas bag in the back, started up the engine and took off.

And that's when I lost my mind. Whether it was

hunger, or my terrible afternoon with Arnold Bromberg, or the fact that I was already a failure at the health club, I don't know. But I temporarily lost my reason and jumped into a red convertible that had paused at the stoplight. "Follow that car!" I cried. "Please! The white one in front of you."

The driver, who was a young guy, started to say something, but I interrupted him. "It's my husband," I said, "and we're in the middle of a custody case. He's stolen my one-year-old child. Please, please follow him!"

Would you believe it? He did as he was told. I mean, he didn't even say boo—just stepped on the gas and began to follow Robert's Jensen Arrow. "I've been looking for him for months," I said. "He's taken my child."

"What a bastard!" said the driver of the car. "Don't worry, miss, we'll overtake him."

"No, no," I said, "just follow at a discreet distance. I need to know where he's living."

"Right," said the young man, "right. What a bastard."

We proceeded through the town of East Hampton, took a few left turns, and wound up on Cobblers' Lane, a street I was not familiar with. Suddenly, Robert's car zipped into a gravel driveway and was obscured by a tall hedge. "This is it," said my driver. "Do you want to get out, or what?"

"I'll get out," I said, "but I won't go in the house. I just want to ascertain the address."

"I'll wait for you," said the young man, making me feel that he was perhaps being *too* helpful. "I'll take you back to town."

Assuring him that I could walk back, I said good-bye to my rescuer, but I could tell that he would have liked to linger. It was obvious that he found the situation very dramatic.

The minute his convertible had disappeared, I stole down the gravel driveway. Keeping close to the hedge, I tiptoed along for a few minutes until Robert's house appeared in the distance. Well, let me tell you. I had expected that he would live in a nice house, but this one was more than nice. It was a brick mansion with green awnings and a circular driveway in front. There were flower gardens everywhere, and—far in the distance— a latticework gazebo. I was floored. Because the whole thing was really posh.

More than posh. What it was, was English. Like some setting out of an English movie where people are always playing croquet on the lawn and sipping cool drinks. The kind of movie where the women wear big straw summer hats, and the men wear ties and blazers. Was Robert Swann an Englishman? It was possible. I mean, I had only heard his voice once, saying "Hi, sweetie," to Betsy, and you couldn't tell anything from that.

I lingered for a moment, looking at this beautiful house and imagining myself living inside it with Robert Swann. I saw myself as a size six, wearing a long chiffon dress and a big hat. I saw Robert and me sitting in the gazebo on summer nights. He was wearing white slacks and a blazer.

I have to explain something to you. Which is that I had never been attracted to the rich before—not once in my life. Because like many of the locals around here, I find the rich very annoying. Every summer they swarm out to Long Island, where they crowd the beaches and where their kids get busted for drunk driving, and then they depart—leaving the rest of us to board up their houses, drain their swimming pools, and protect their property over the winter. The local merchants are half crazed while they are here—marking their merchandise way up, trying to make a buck—only to collapse after Labor Day, when all of this expensive junk goes on sale. Etc.

Anyway, Robert was nowhere to be seen. His car had been left in the driveway, but he was gone. Reluctantly, I stole back to the main road, feeling both excited and frustrated. Then a little girl strolled toward me, eating a lollipop. She was around eight years old. "Excuse me," I said. "Yeah?" she said. "What?"

"Do you live around here?"

She eyed me coolly, still licking her lollipop. "Yeah. Next door."

"Well then, could you give me some information?"

A canny look came over her face. "Maybe. What'll you give me for it?"

I fished around in my gym bag and found fifty cents. "Fifty cents?" I suggested.

"Make it a dollar and you've got a deal."

I found a dollar and gave it to her. "What do you wanna know?" she said.

"Well . . . something about your neighbors. The Swanns."

"Oh, them. They're boring. They never *do* anything."

"Go on," I said.

The kid took a few more licks of her lollipop. "Mr. Swann works in the city, on Wall Street. Mrs. Swann gives a lot of tea parties. It's dull."

"And the son?" I prompted. "Robert? What about him?"

She shrugged. "I don't know. He has a lot of girlfriends. He goes out a lot. Are you a detective?"

"No. I'm just doing some research on the families in this neighborhood. For a book. Actually, I'm an author."

The kid finished her lollipop and threw the stick away.

"Will you put me in the book?" she asked.

"Absolutely. I'll make you one of the characters. What else does Robert do?"

She thought for a moment. "Well, he plays tennis and goes to the beach, and stuff like that. He has an Irish setter named Chauncy."

"Yes?"

"He skis," said the child, "in Switzerland sometimes. That's all."

"Thank you," I said to her. "That's very helpful."

"Will you really put me in the book?"

"Absolutely," I declared. "What's your name?"

"Hilda Wertheimer," she replied. And then we parted.

I hitched a ride back to town with a woman in a station wagon, and arrived in front of the health club just before my mother did. And as she drove me back to Sag Harbor, she kept asking why I was so quiet. Had my first day at the club been all right, she wanted to know. Did I meet anyone nice. Yes, yes, I kept saying. But my mind was on Robert—putting the pieces of his life together as though I were indeed, as Nicole always said, a fat spy. Girlfriends and the beach. Tennis and an Irish setter. Switzerland. That part threw me, because I had no idea how I would ever get to Switzerland, much less learn to ski. Then I realized that I hadn't asked the girl the one question that was important to me—which was whether or not Robert was English. He had to be, I thought. No one who wasn't English would live in a house like that.

8

I HAD LOST TWO POUNDS. Hard to believe, but that's what the scale said. Two pounds, count them, two. And while you may be thinking that two pounds is not a big deal, it was to me. Because it had been years since I had lost anything at all. I was sticking to a diet called the Take-It-Off-Fast Diet, invented by a woman named Monica Briar, and it was working. No matter that I sometimes fainted and hallucinated on this diet. No matter that I had to pee all the time because of the ten glasses of water I was drinking each day. I had only been dieting for one week and was beginning to lose. Nicole was amazed, my parents were amazed. And I was proud.

I began to pause in front of shop windows and stare at clothes—the kind of clothes I had never worn in my life. Tiny little outfits made of bright cottons and silks. Loose-knit white sweaters. Toreador pants. Knee britches worn with white stockings and patent leather shoes. Someday, I said to myself, *you* will be wearing clothes like that. Someday you will be skiing in Switzerland.

I bought a book on Switzerland and a book on Irish setters. I looked up the Swanns in the Manhattan phone book and discovered that they lived on Fifth Avenue and 85th Street. I went to the club every day and watched Robert work out, and swim, and drive away in his Jensen Arrow—but I didn't speak to him. The time wasn't right yet. I had to be thinner, more attractive, more poised.

However. There is a lot you can learn about a person from just watching him, and during the next week I learned a lot about Robert. Such as the fact that he was very good-humored and patient. Such as the fact that he swam like a champion. He had never once noticed me, or cast his eyes my way, so I began to grow bolder in observing him. One day I even sat by the pool, wearing one of my mumus, and watched him do laps. His concentration was fantastic. I mean, he looked like something out of the Olympics. Back and forth, back and forth across the pool he went, his blond hair slicked back and dark with water, his eyes that startling blue.

I watched him use the Nautilus machines. I watched him ride the stationary bicycles. And if I could have watched him getting a massage—all naked and gorgeous and tan—I would have done that too. But of course, the massage rooms were private. I followed him one day to the health food store in East Hampton, where he bought a bottle of vitamin B capsules. I stood outside a record store while he browsed. Some days he wore his little navy shorts, and on other days burgundy jogging pants. And of course, there were often girls with him. Not one particular girl, just a lot of different girls—strolling along with him, chatting with him, being given lifts in his car. But, strangely enough, I wasn't jealous. It would have been odd if there *hadn't* been girls around Robert Swann.

I went back to Overeaters Anonymous. And this was a big step for me, because I hate OA. Don't get me wrong. It is a superb organization and a wonderful support group, but the only group in my neighborhood is filled with a lot of older women who talk about nothing but sex. Their main preoccupation is this. If they get thin, truly thin, will they be raped? Will their husbands find them so irresistible that they will never give them a moment's peace? Will strange men pull them into alleyways? Will they be in danger for the rest of their lives? Nevertheless. I went to the meetings and listened to these women talk about the dangers of being thin. And I kept on dieting.

Nicole was preoccupied these days with Norman the bullfighter and their wonderful new relationship. But she tried to make time for me. We took a lot of walks on the beach, and phoned each other every night. And if I did go into the Heavenly Cafe, I ate only salads and diet drinks, and cottage cheese and fruit. Nicole was really impressed with my determination, and, because she kept pestering me about Robert, I finally told her what I knew about him. Which wasn't much. But I had gone back to the brick mansion one afternoon, around five-thirty, and had concealed myself once more by the hedge. For a long while the house had been quiet. Then two beautiful women had emerged from the front door and gone to sit on the veranda in wicker chairs. I knew at once that they were Robert's mother and grandmother, and don't ask me how I knew. I just did. The mother was blond, like Robert, and fairly young. But the grandmother was a knockout. Tall and thin, with gorgeous white hair and beautiful summer clothes. They sat there on the porch together, drinking cool drinks, and when they were finished a maid came out and got the glasses. It was like a scene from that television series *Brideshead Revisited*.

"How do you know the older one was the grandmother?" Nicole asked me. We were sitting on the Bridgehampton beach, watching the waves roll in to shore, and it was a Wednesday afternoon.

"I just know," I said to her. "And I saw the dog, too. Chauncy. He was running around chasing a rubber ball."

Nicole ran a hand through her mop of hair. "But my darling mouse, this spying will get you nowhere. What you must do is speak to the man, make chums with him."

55

"I can't, Nicole. Not till I'm thin."

"But doesn't this man, this Robert, ever notice you?"

"No, not yet. Not really."

Nicole lit a cigaret, cupping her hands around the match. "It is one crazy situation, I tell you. You love a man, you *take* a man. You do not hover in the background."

"That's fine for you to say," I said, surprising myself with the grief I suddenly felt. "You're beautiful."

Nicole thought for a moment. "I am no more beautiful than anyone else. I simply work on myself. I work on hair, figure, and makeup. I learn how to make the love most satisfying. And you could do the same."

"Not till I'm thin. I've got to be thin first."

"I have it!" she said. "I have a solution! I will join this club too, and then there will be three of us. You will use me as the bait to catch the fish."

I was really startled. "What?"

Nicole stubbed out her cigaret and looked intently at me. "I will join the club and make friends with this man. And because you are my chum, you will make friends with him too. There will be three of us! And then, *I* will disappear and leave the two of you desperately together. What do you think?"

I was amazed. I mean, this was the one thing I had never considered. And what a dangerous idea it was! Because suppose Robert and Nicole liked each other, or even fell in love? No, I reasoned, that wouldn't happen because of Norman the bullfighter. Nicole was deeply in love with him and didn't want anyone else. She had told me this a hundred times.

"Let me think about it," I said. "Let me consider it for a while."

"OK, OK, you consider," she replied. "But believe me, this is a good plan. I will make myself the bait to catch the fish. I will do this out of love for you."

I looked at Nicole and realized that she did love me. It was amazing, but she did. And then it occurred to me that she was the best friend anyone could have. I had had close friends before, but this was something different. This was devotion.

"You're wonderful," I said to her. "But let me think about it for a while."

She lay back in the sand and sighed. "Men," she said. "Women. It is the bafflement of all time."

IT WAS TWO DAYS LATER and I was sitting in the back of the dog grooming parlor with Arnold Bromberg. There had been no orders for cheesecake that day, and so we were having coffee together and chatting. Fortunately, he had not offered me any cheesecake because the supply was low. There was some beautiful music playing on the stereo, which turned out to be Bach. An oratorio. "I'm writing a book on Bach," said Arnold Bromberg. "In my spare time."

"No kidding?" I said. "You're a busy man, Mr. Bromberg."

"It's true," he replied. "I have, perhaps, too much on my plate—but nonetheless I am grateful. Grateful for my life and my work. And grateful for you too, Miss Formica, if I may say so."

I blushed—which seemed to be something I did frequently in Arnold's presence. "Thank you for the nice words," I said.

"They are utterly true, Miss Formica. And by the way, if I may mention this, haven't you lost some weight?"

I blushed again, surprised that he had noticed. "Well yes, I have. A few pounds."

"It is terribly becoming," said Arnold Bromberg.

To cover my confusion, I took my coffee cup over to the stove and poured myself another cup. In the few weeks that I had worked for Arnold, we had received pitifully few orders, but when an order had come in the other day, for three cakes, I had decided not to take any more chances on the bicycle. Pretending to leave on that vehicle, I had ditched it in a bush two blocks away and phoned for a taxicab. The cab had cost ten dollars to Bridgehampton round trip, but it had been worth it because the cheesecakes arrived intact. This time, the woman who received them was nice and said that the cakes looked fine. The trouble was that I was spending more on the job than I was earning. And Arnold, in turn, was paying me more than *he* was earning. It was a peculiar situation.

"Tell me about your book," I said, as I brought my coffee back to the table. "What's it about?"

Arnold thought for a moment, giving me time to study him. He was wearing a blue business suit that was shiny with age, but he still looked immaculate—his curly hair neatly brushed, his fingernails manicured.

"I can't really tell you what the book is about," he said. "Oh, I suppose I could say that it is about the life of Johann Sebastian Bach, and what he did to augment organ music. But that wouldn't be the whole of it. You see, Miss Formica, the book I am writing is about Bach only on the surface. Deep down, it is about man's relationship to the universe. I have always found the universe to be benevolent, and the bad things that happen in life merely grains of sand upon a beach of heaven."

I was so surprised that I couldn't speak. Because I had never realized that Arnold was so intellectual. Grains of sand upon a beach of heaven was a terrific phrase, really,

59

but I wasn't sure what it meant. "Go on," I said, because that was all I could think of saying.

Arnold stared into space. "You may think that these preoccupations come from my having been a minister's son, but not at all. I have known from the day I was born that there is a universal mind, and that it is totally benevolent. Right action, so to speak, is always taking place. It is only the little minds of men that think differently."

I considered this for a moment. To me, the universe was just a big blob surrounding us all. With a few trillion stars scattered about. "I'm not sure I agree with you," I said.

Arnold waved his hand toward the bookcases that lined the room. "Every man is his own philosopher. I mean, just look at whom we have over there. Brandt and Spinoza, Heidegger and Weil. Jung. Swedenborg."

I had never heard of any of these people, but I didn't want him to know it. "Right," I said. "Absolutely."

Arnold laughed self-consciously. "Enough of me. Tell me something about yourself. You have looked so radiant these past days, Miss Formica. So fulfilled."

Fulfilled? Physically, I was dying of hunger—and mentally, I was dying of love. How could I look fulfilled? "Well," I said, "I have been losing some weight, and working out at the club in East Hampton. I guess that's what you notice."

"Stay with the diet," said Arnold. "Persevere. You can do it, you know, and the results will be wonderful. Your full beauty will emerge."

Again, I blushed—this time to the roots of my hair. "Thank you," I murmured.

Arnold looked embarrassed. "Forgive me for being personal. If I grow too personal, you must tell me."

"That's OK, Mr. Bromberg. Really." And then there was a pause.

I wanted to ask him questions. About his childhood in Kansas, and his father the minister, and—most of all—how he supported himself. I know this was a crass thought, in the midst of a conversation about the universe, but it bothered me. Was Arnold independently wealthy? Was his father a *rich* minister?

"Are you happy here?" I asked instead. "In Sag Harbor."

Arnold finished the last drop of his coffee. "Yes. I am as happy as I have ever been in my life. To live in this beautiful place is a dream fulfilled for me. The ocean, the bay, the harbors . . . And the shorebirds, Miss Formica! The herons and egrets and swans! Once they were only pictures in a book to me—now they are real."

"But aren't you lonely?" I asked, regretting at once that I had said it. It was probably too personal a thing to say.

Arnold smiled. "How could a man as fortunate as

myself be lonely? I have my book and my music. I have my goat Daisy, who, by the way, I would like you to meet someday. And I have my friendship with you, Miss Formica. If I may say so."

Another silence descended on us. "Why don't you call me Rita?" I said. "I mean, don't you think Miss Formica is a little formal?"

"I will call you Rita if you will call me Arnold," he replied. "Tit for tat."

Fantastic, I thought. After two long weeks, we are about to go onto a first-name basis. "I get lonely sometimes," I admitted. "But I shouldn't. Not with my parents so devoted to me and everything—and not with my friend Nicole around."

"There is solitude and there is loneliness," said Arnold, "and they are different things. Solitude is a kind of grace, a connection with the universe. Loneliness, on the other hand, is mere dissatisfaction. A longing for the things one does not have."

I knew instantly what he meant. "Have you ever heard of Lily Tomlin?" I asked.

"I'm afraid not. Is she a poet?"

"No, she's an actress. And one of the things she said once, in a one-woman show, was that reality is nothing but a collective hunch."

I thought this was funny, and I expected him to laugh, but he didn't. "That is a very wise statement," he said.

For the third time, a silence overtook us. But this time it was a prolonged one. "I guess I should go home," I said, "if there aren't any orders today. What are *you* going to do? For the rest of the afternoon."

Arnold smiled his nine-year-old smile. "I thought I would walk over to that pond by the bay beach. And look for egrets."

It sounded like a nice idea, and in a funny way I would have liked to go with him. But I didn't suggest it. I mean, Arnold Bromberg was turning out to be the greatest loner I had ever met, and I had the feeling that he could spend the rest of his life in solitude—not loneliness—without minding it at all. Unlike me, who was so obsessed with Robert that I wanted to die at times, Arnold could find total happiness looking for egrets.

"Are egrets white?" I asked, feeling a little foolish. Because I felt this was something I should have known.

"Pure white," he replied, "and very large, like the great blue herons. They are completely solitary. Except when breeding, of course."

Aren't we all? I thought.

Arnold walked me out to the porch and extended his hand. I shook it, but for some reason I didn't leave. We just stood there looking at each other. He opened his mouth to speak, and I thought he was going to say something about egrets, but instead he said, "Miss Formica, do you know where I could rent an organ?"

For one second I thought he meant a heart or a kidney. Then I realized he was talking about organ as in musical instrument. "Gee," I said. "I don't."

He sighed. "That's all right. It's just that I am used to playing the organ, and I can't seem to find one around here."

"I'll give it some thought," I said to him. "Goodbye, Mr. Bromberg."

10

IT HAD BEEN SIXTEEN DAYS since I had first seen Robert on the streets of East Hampton, and I had lost five pounds. But the private dossier I was keeping on the Swanns was still meager. I could find out nothing more about Robert save that he came and went from the club, that he had many girlfriends, and that his tan was changing from pale gold to dark honey. I had heard his voice now, and knew that he was not English. I had discovered his secret passion—gumdrops. But I had still not spoken to him, and whenever our paths crossed at the club he looked right through me. Very few people do this— because of my size—but as far as Robert was concerned,

I didn't exist. My mother kept asking me how I was doing at the club, and I kept saying fine, fine—but it wasn't the truth. I was an absolute failure as far as "participation" went, and participation, Betsy kept telling me, was the name of the game.

Meanwhile, summer had descended on the Hamptons in its usual gruesome way. What I mean is, summer is an interlude that we locals have to grit our teeth and endure. Route 27, which is the artery to the Long Island Expressway, becomes so congested that motorists have been known to leave their cars and phone the cops for help—lest they spend their whole weekend in a traffic jam. And then there are the grocery stores, which become so crowded that you practically have to go shopping at dawn—and then there are the beaches, which are filled with raucous kids. Only a person like Arnold Bromberg, I thought, would find summer in the Hamptons beautiful. To the rest of us, the season was a trial.

It was about this time—sixteen days after I had first seen Robert—that I decided to go for diet counseling at the club. I had been doing well on my diet, miraculously well, but then an odd thing happened. Strolling through East Hampton one day, hoping that I might see Robert on the street, I passed the Knave of Hearts Bakery and came to a dead halt. Because the entire bakery window was filled with strawberry shortcakes. Not one, not five,

65

but dozens and dozens of strawberry shortcakes. There were so many of them that I felt I had fallen into a bad dream, that in the midst of sanity I was about to go crazy. I really have a thing about strawberries, and here was this shop window bursting, swimming, *vibrating* with strawberry shortcakes. All freshly baked. All scrumptious. And so I faltered.

Falter isn't the truth. What happened is that I walked into the bakery like someone in a trance, took some money from my purse, and bought a strawberry short-cake. Only when I was out on the street again, did I realize what I had done—and then, as sanity returned, I didn't know what to do with the cake. It seemed criminal to throw it away, and yet I knew if I ate it, I would be lost. Finished. Ruined. So I walked up to a fat man on the street, who was looking into the bookstore window, and handed him the cake. "Happy birthday," I said.

I ran the two blocks to the club and hurried up to Betsy, who was at the desk. "Where's the diet counselor?" I said to her. "You know. The one who works here."

Betsy gave me one of her usual looks. "You have to sign up," she said. "The appointment sheet is on the bulletin board."

So I rushed over to the bulletin board and saw that

under the words "Diet Counseling" there were two appointments left that day. I wrote my name in the slot that said "four P.M.," sat down, and waited.

At exactly four P.M. the door to the diet counselor's room opened and a man walked out. The door closed again, and feeling extremely nervous, I went over and knocked. "Yes?" said a voice from within. I opened the door a crack. "I'm your next appointment," I said. "May I come in?"

The woman who greeted me was around forty years old, very sallow-looking, and was dressed in a linen suit and high heels. City clothes. And as I contemplated her, I saw that she was thin, homely, and humorless. Don't ask me how I knew she was humorless—I just knew. "Uh, my name is Skylar Cunningham," I said. "I need some counseling."

The woman got up from her desk, walked over to me and extended her hand. "My name is Marsha Strawberry. How do you do?"

We sat down facing each other, Miss Strawberry looking expectant, and me, I guess, looking stunned. Marsha Strawberry, I said to myself, Marsha Strawberry. I don't believe it.

Miss Strawberry took out a pencil and pad. "How much do you weigh?" she asked me. I told her. "And what is your height?" she inquired. I told her that too.

"Now," she declared, putting her pencil down, "let's share with one another. Let's talk."

I wasn't sure what she wanted me to talk about, but in the next few minutes I managed to reveal my eating history, all the different diets I had been on, and the diet I was on at the moment. I told her about my very nice life and my very nice parents, transporting all of us, including the dog, to Southampton. The Cunninghams.

I had been doing a lot of work on Skylar Cunningham during the past week, inventing clothes for her, deciding where she lived—an estate near the ocean—and creating a dignified past. Private school, Europe in the summers, stuff like that. Skylar Cunningham had had a nanny until she was ten yers old and spoke perfect French. Her coming-out party would be at the Hotel Pierre, in New York.

Miss Strawberry was nodding patiently. "First of all," she said, "there is psychological hunger and there is stomach hunger, and they are not the same thing."

"True," I said, because that was all I could think of saying.

"You must learn what you are hungry *for*," she declared. "Because, of course, it isn't food."

Sorry lady, I said in the privacy of my mind, but it *is* food. I am hungry, hungry, hungry for food. Strawberries in particular. And your last name isn't helping me.

"Estrangement from the body makes it hard to be receptive to proper hunger signals," Marsha Strawberry said, "and this distortion of the hunger mechanism begins early in life—a way of meeting needs that have nothing to do with food at all. It is not food that you are longing for, Skylar, it is identity."

"It is?" I said.

"Think of your fat as an attempt to pursue an individual life," said Marsha Strawberry. "Think of it as a way of breaking the bond with your mother.

"There are two people inside you," Miss Strawberry continued. "A fat person and a thin person—a young woman who longs for identity, and an infant who thinks that food means love. We must kill the infant and strengthen the woman. Don't you agree?"

"No," I said, "I don't. I mean, to begin with, the idea of killing an infant is sort of horrible—if you'll excuse me for saying so. And secondly, my mother and I are very separate people. We go our own ways."

Miss Strawberry gave me a cold look. "Are you disagreeing with me, Skylar?"

"Well . . ." I said.

Miss Strawberry was turning from cold to frigid. "Because if you are, then I don't think we can work together."

"Actually . . ."

"I have counseled hundreds of young women," said

69

Marsha Strawberry, "and my methods have brought results. I am a Ph.D., Skylar, trained for this work, and it is only modesty that keeps me from using the title of 'Doctor.' I could be 'Doctor Strawberry' any day of the week, but I choose not to use the title because I choose not to intimidate my clients. Is that clear?"

"Yes, ma'am," I said. "I mean, yes Doctor. Sure. Of course."

Marsha Strawberry relaxed a little. "Very well, then. Let us discuss the fat you, and the thin you, and who they really are."

On and on. For an hour, a whole hour. The fat me and the thin me, my identity problem and my attachment to my mother. My fear of *rivaling* my mother. Food as a drug and a potion, food as daydreaming and escape. The dangers of food, the seductiveness of food. Alienation from the body, regression and sublimation. God! In the first place, I had heard it all before—though not in so complicated a form. And in the second place, what I wanted to talk about was simply how to avoid bakery windows filled with strawberry shortcakes. But we never got to that.

At the end of the session Marsha Strawberry gave me two assignments. One was to write down my thoughts about food every day, in a kind of stream of consciousness, and the other was to practice Thin Hours. Thin

Hours were hours when I was to behave like a thin person. Fat Hours, I guess, were all the rest.

Against my better judgment, I made an appointment with Miss Strawberry for the following week. We shook hands, parted grimly, and I left her dark little room. Blinking in the fluorescent light of the outer room, where the Nautilus equipment was, I saw Robert Swann. He was wearing a pair of navy-blue swimming trunks and had a towel over his shoulder.

Watching him head for the pool, dressed in the tiniest of bathing suits, his skin the color of honey, his hair the color of pale wheat, seeing this apparition pass me and realizing all over again that I had never even spoken to him, that he didn't know I existed . . . seeing and realizing all this made me feel desperate. Without stopping to consider what I was doing, I rushed into the women's locker room and put on my bathing suit. I would introduce myself to Robert Swann in the swimming pool. I would slip into the water unobtrusively, and then, with the aqua-green liquid disguising my shape, strike up a conversation. You did not always see people's bodies in swimming pools. The bodies were blurred by water. What you saw were heads, eyes, and smiles. And Nicole had told me a thousand times that I had a pretty face and a wonderful smile. Slipping my pink mumu over my suit, I headed for the pool. Dear God, I prayed—

forgetting that I was an atheist—please let him like me. If you will just let him like me, I will never ask for anything again.

11

ROBERT SWANN was already doing laps when I arrived. Back and forth, back and forth he went, his body like a god's, his determination like a scientist's. There was no one else in the water and he was taking advantage of it. Back and forth, back and forth—tossing the water from his eyes, his strokes perfect, his breathing regular and controlled. He looked macho and refined, intelligent and athletic. Simultaneously.

On my way down the corridor to the pool, I had planned my strategy. I would stand near the diving board in my mumu, and then, with split-second timing, I would toss the mumu over my head and dive into the water. He would not see my body. He would only see the splash, and then I would be in the pool with him, ready to make his acquaintance, ready to introduce myself as Skylar Cunningham. I lived in Southampton and spent most of my summers in Europe. I had had a nanny until I was ten. I would be coming out at the Pierre.

I stood near the diving board, my heart pounding in my chest. I watched Robert cutting back and forth through the water. I said another prayer and gauged my distances. I watched Robert again. I took hold of the mumu, my hands holding it out on either side, as though I were about to curtsy. Now! I said to myself. Now! Go, jump, dive!

I dove—straight down into the aqua water. Only something went wrong in the moment that I tried to throw the mumu over my head, because it didn't throw. What it did was wind around my neck in a spiraling motion, sort of like a noose. As I hit the water, it was choking me. Suddenly I was drowning with a pale-pink mumu wrapped around my neck. "Help!" I screamed.

In one second, Robert was by my side. "Don't panic!" he yelled. "I'll get you." But I was flailing like a wounded whale, the mumu growing tighter and tighter. Robert grabbed me and I spat a stream of water into his face. "Relax!" he yelled, as he put his arm around me in a lifeguard's grip. "Relax, goddammit!" As I kicked and gasped, and tried to loosen the mumu from my neck, he dragged me to shore.

A second later, Robert Swann and I were facing each other—poolside. He looked angry, and how I looked, I do not want to imagine. The mumu was still wound around my neck and my horrid bathing suit had crawled up my hips, exposing my thighs. "Are you all right?"

he asked, but he didn't look friendly. "Fine," I sputtered, "fine. I'm perfectly fine."

He led me over to a bench and we sat down together. I tried to loosen the mumu, but it was still—forever, perhaps—wrapped around my neck. Robert wiped the water from his face. "What were you *doing*?" he asked. "What happened?"

I decided to ignore the question. And, struggling for some kind of dignity, I said, "Thank you very much."

He glared at me. "That's OK. What were you doing in there?"

"Swimming," I said. "Allow me to introduce myself. Skylar Formica."

It was a terrible blunder, but I couldn't retrieve it. The words were out. "I'm Robert Swann," he declared.

We sat there for a moment—Robert with the water streaming from his body, and me with the mumu around my neck and one bathing suit strap sliding down. I tried to hitch it up, aware of how huge my breasts must look.

Robert rose to his feet. "Well," he said, "if you're all right, Miss . . ."

"Cunningham."

He looked at me oddly. "Miss Cunningham," he repeated. "If you're all right now, I'll be going."

"Must you?" I said, trying to sound social and pleasant.

He gave me another odd look. "See you around," he said.

I sat there for a long time after he had gone, aware of my size, my weight, the mumu around my neck, my huge breasts and fat legs—aware of the total ugliness I represented in this world, the total klutziness I personified in a universe of beautiful people like Robert Swann—and then I went to phone Nicole.

12

I WAS EATING AGAIN—blueberry pancakes and strawberry malteds. Strawberry malteds and cheeseburgers deluxe. Oreo cookies, pizza, Gummy Bears. I *thought* I was dieting but I wasn't, which just goes to show you the split personality of the junkie. I am dieting, I would say to myself, as I starved through an entire morning. Then I would rush to an ice cream parlor and have a malt. I am dieting, I assured myself, as I skipped lunch—only to wind up at a grocery store buying potato chips. You are crazy, one voice would say to me, you are blowing the whole damn thing. No, another voice would answer, I'm just hungry. I deserve to be fed.

That awful Strawberry woman had been right. There were two people inside me, and the hungry one seemed to be winning. Skylar Cunningham was being vanquished by Rita Formica. I did my stream-of-consciousness writing in preparation for my next session with Miss Strawberry. I practiced Thin Hours, only to have them turn into Fat Hours right away. To everyone in the world, except Nicole, I appeared to be on a diet. But I had gained three pounds.

I had phoned Nicole from the club that day—the day of the mumu incident—and told her that I was ready to accept her proposal. "I've hit bottom," I said to her. "I really have."

"The bottom of what?" she inquired.

"My life," I replied. "The mumu did it."

Nicole groaned. "Mouse dear, the mumu—it is not for you at all. A bad style."

"You should have told me that earlier," I said.

And so, the next afternoon, she had come to the club with me and signed up for a month's membership. She got off work at three, and would drive me to the club every day after my job, if that's what you could call it, with Mr. Bromberg.

Well, let me tell you. Nicole's entrance into the world of fitness was noticed by everyone. By Betsy, who brightened up the minute she saw her, and also by Robert Swann. Dressed in shocking-pink tights and a black leotard, her gorgeous hair piled high upon her head, Nicole swept into the place like a movie star. "I am Nicole Sicard," she announced to everyone in the Nautilus room. "I have come here to do the workouts, to become fit."

In one second, Nicole had a crowd around her. People were welcoming her to the club, Betsy was chatting away, the male fitness instructors were buzzing around like flies—and at a distance stood Robert Swann. His eyes went over Nicole from head to toe, appreciating every inch of her body, appreciating the pink tights and black leotard, the little black ballet slippers she was wearing, her subtle makeup, her mop of beautiful hair. He looked at her like an art critic who has just seen a masterpiece.

Nicole didn't need to have Robert pointed out to her. She knew who he was at once, and in the most charming way she glided over to him. "I am Nicole," she said sweetly, "and I have come here to do the workouts. Only, I do not understand this place at all. Will you show me the ropes, Mr. . . ."

"Swann," said Robert eagerly. "Sure. I'll be glad to."

Leaving Betsy behind, Robert proceeded to give Nicole the grand tour. At a discreet distance I followed, my heart thumping with excitement. It was working just as Nicole and I had planned. The only trouble was that Robert didn't seem to know I was there. Having saved my life but a day earlier, he looked right through me as the three of us toured the club. When we reached the swimming pool, Nicole paused and stared at the water. "Oh, such a big pool," she sighed. "And me, I do not swim."

"I'll teach you," Robert said quickly. "Will you let me teach you?"

She batted her eyes at him. "Would you do that for me? I never swim. I have this fear."

"I have a certificate in swimming instruction," Robert said firmly.

She smiled at him like a beautiful, helpless child. "You will not let me drown?"

Robert grinned. "No way."

"I depend always on the kindness of strangers," Nicole breathed. "And they never disappoint me."

I could have been invisible, for all the impact I was making on this scene. And yet, I wasn't threatened because I could see that Nicole was acting. Even "the kindness of strangers" was a quote from somewhere, a Tennessee Williams play, I think. Nicole, I said silently, you are a genius.

We continued around the club, Robert explaining everything and me remaining invisible. He took Nicole through the whole sequence of the Nautilus machines and then he invited her out for coffee. I was still standing there with them, invisible to everyone in the universe but myself, but I tried to remain calm. All this is for a purpose, I told myself. Nicole is the key that will open the door.

I have to admit that I felt funny as the two of them left the club together. And I have to admit that my heart sank as, with a courtly gesture, Robert ushered her out of the place. However, at the last second, Nicole turned around and gave me a little wink—and that made me know I was safe. "Trust me, darling mouse," said the wink. "I am only the bait to catch the fish."

She phoned me that night and told me what had happened. She and Robert had gone to The Beautiful Bean, a coffeehouse in East Hampton, and had talked for two hours. Then he had driven her home. I myself had struggled home on the bus and was a little resentful about this, a little resentful about everything as a matter of fact, but Nicole soothed me right away. "How can you like this man?" she said to me. "He is so boring."

"Boring!" I said. "What do you mean, boring?"

There was a sigh on the other end of the phone. "My darling mouse, this man is nothing but a jock. All he talks about is the workout, and the fitness, and the swimming. He never read a book, he never go to films. He is a jock! What do you find so interesting?"

I thought for a moment. "It isn't a question of finding him interesting. I love him."

Nicole sputtered with exasperation. "I do this for you,

but I am already bored with the whole thing. He invite me for a date on Tuesday night, and do you know where? To a boxing match."

I thought of Norman the bullfighter. "But Norman's physical too. And you're crazy about him."

"That is a different matter. Norman, he fight *bulls*, he put his life on the line, he show courage. Your Robert is nothing but a jock."

"Stick with it," I said to her. "Please, Nicole. I need you."

"OK, OK," she said impatiently. "I date him a few times, and then I bring you along with us. Pretty soon, I drop out. I am already bored."

I hung up the phone with a whole bag of mixed feelings. Relief that Nicole did not find Robert attractive. Amazement that she thought he was boring. Confusion, as usual, over Norman's bullfighting career in Brooklyn. Loneliness, pain, hunger, and not a little bit of despair. I went to my closet and retrieved a Sara Lee cake that I had hidden in a suitcase. After locking my door, I ate the whole thing.

Nicole went to the boxing match with Robert, and after that he took her to a baseball game. And after every date she would phone me to protest. "Boring!" she said to me. "He is so boring. Why do I do this for you?"

"Because you love me," I replied. "And I love you

too. I swear to you, Nicole, I'll pay you back someday. Truly."

Meanwhile, I continued to eat. My Thin Hours were vanishing into Thin Seconds, and my stream-of-consciousness writing was becoming very dark, very depressed. Every day Nicole and I would drive over to the club, and every day I would watch Robert growing more and more attracted to her. Bravely, Nicole would try to introduce me into the conversation. Bravely, she would try to explain that she and I were friends. "Skylar, she and I meet in Paris years ago," she said to Robert at one point. "Skylar and me are old chums."

Robert looked at me in a glazed sort of way, seeing only the fat person he had recently rescued from drowning—not a world traveler. "Oh," he said, "yes, of course. Paris. Very nice."

He had only spoken to me once in all these days, by the pool, and that was to say, "Would you hand me a towel?" It wasn't much of a sentence, but I clung to it. He had spoken to me. He had asked me for a towel.

Before a week had gone by, Nicole knew everything about Robert. He read sports magazines. The only thing he watched on TV was baseball. His favorite food was porterhouse steak. He never ate ice cream. He took several showers a day and had a whole wardrobe of workout clothes. He was a car buff and could often be found working under the hood of his car. Boring, said Nicole, boring. But to me, these morsels of information were confirming something Nicole was not aware of. She saw only the surface of Robert Swann. What *I* saw was something different.

I was sure of it now. Beneath the jocklike surface of Robert Swann another person lived. A person who was lonely, like myself. A sensitive man who could never show his sensitivity—and who thus pretended to be an all-American guy. The Other Robert probably loved classical music and went to museums. The Other Robert took long lonely walks on the beach. The health club, the foreign cars, the girlfriends—these were only a front for something deep and beautiful. For all I knew, Robert Swann wrote poetry at night. For all any of us knew, he was afraid of women.

Crazy, crazy. The more Nicole dated Robert, the more I fell in love with him. Hovering around the fringes of their relationship, I waited and watched, wrote more about him in my Swann Dossier, and kept on eating. My penchant for making up stories had never been greater, as I invented scenarios in which Robert and I flew, in a private jet, to the Swiss Alps. I saw us in Paris and Rome, wandering the narrow streets. I saw us lounging on the Riviera. In these daydreams I was always thin, of course, and Nicole was totally absent. In one scenario I actually had her dead, with Robert and me standing by the grave-side, but I changed that one immediately. I loved Nicole and did not want her dead. She was the best friend a person could ever have.

13

ARNOLD BROMBERG AND I were sitting in a marsh by a little pond, waiting for egrets to fly by. Business being slow that day, he had suggested that we go birdwatch-ing, and I had agreed. So here we were, loaded down with binoculars and bird books and mosquito spray—sitting in a damp marsh on a steaming afternoon. There is no place as humid as the Hamptons in summer, but Arnold didn't seem to be aware of it. He was looking through his binoculars.

Arnold was wearing a pair of blue jeans, sneakers, and a checked shirt—and almost looked normal. As for me, I was wearing a pair of overalls and a T-shirt. Ten days had gone by since Nicole and Robert had met each other, and I was very depressed. The plan wasn't work-ing at all, but I didn't know what to do about it. I had set this whole thing into motion, and now I had to endure. "Do you see anything?" I asked Mr. Bromberg.

"Only a swan," he said. "Over there, near the little island."

I wished that he had not used the word "swan," but I couldn't say anything about it. "Do you really think we'll see an egret?"

"Of course we will, Miss Formica. It's only a matter of time. And I assure you that when we do see one, you will be thrilled."

Guess again, I thought. But since I didn't want to hurt his feelings, I said, "You really love birds, Mr. Bromberg, don't you?"

Arnold took the binocula.s from his eyes. "Yes, I do love them. But I love all animals. You must come with me one Sunday and meet Daisy, my goat."

The idea of meeting Arnold's goat Daisy depressed me so much that I could have committed suicide. Here I was, sitting in a marsh with Mr. Bromberg, discussing goats, when Robert and Nicole were at a polo match together. Laughing, joking, sipping cool drinks.

As Arnold put the binoculars to his face again, I thought some more about suicide. Maybe that was the way out for me, the way to put an end to my longing for Robert Swann. If I died young, I would not have to screw up my life. People would remember me with sadness and respect.

Mr. Bromberg was no longer looking through his

binoculars. He was looking at me. "What's wrong?" I asked.

"Nothing, Miss Formica. It's just that you seem so sad today, so forlorn."

My eyes filled with tears. If he had said something sharp or critical, I would have been OK. But his kindness hurt me. "It's nothing. Really."

"I don't want to pry," said Arnold Bromberg, "but I have sensed a great sadness in you these days, and it has worried me. Is there anything I can do to help?"

To change the subject, I pointed at a bird who was flying by. "Is that an egret?"

"No, no, just a gull. But an egret will come by soon, I promise you. . . . Can you tell me what's wrong?"

Suddenly I decided to take a chance on Arnold Bromberg. Don't ask me why, but I felt that I could trust him. I mean, he was weird and eccentric and all that, but he did seem interested.

"I'm in love," I said to him. "And it's killing me."

An odd expression came over his face—one that I assumed to be disapproval—but the die was cast. "His name is Robert Swann and he lives in East Hampton," I continued. "He's a very sensitive blond athlete. I love him."

"Oh, dear," said Mr. Bromberg. "How very difficult. Because your words imply that he does not reciprocate."

"Reciprocate?" I said in a choked voice. "He doesn't know I'm alive."

I told Arnold Bromberg the entire story. How I had dropped my mother's dry cleaning in a heap the moment I had seen Robert, and how I had followed him into the club. How I had joined the club, and started to diet, and gone for counseling. And how, finally, I had set Nicole as the bait to catch the fish. The part about Nicole embarrassed me, but now that I had started I couldn't stop. Arnold Bromberg was probably a virgin and had never felt the stirrings of sex in his entire life. But what the hell. I needed to confide in someone.

"So you see what a mess it is," I concluded. "As bait, Nicole is working perfectly. But Robert still doesn't know I'm alive. And Nicole is getting testy about the whole thing because of Norman the bullfighter. It's a goddam mess."

Arnold Bromberg took out a clean white handkerchief and began to polish his binoculars. After a moment, he said, "I find it utterly baffling that this fellow doesn't notice you."

"Why?"

"Because you are such a charming person! I mean, my goodness, what a fool the man must be."

Well, let me tell you. I was very touched. But I could see that Arnold didn't understand the situation at all. He was completely unworldly—like a choirboy. And I was sure he was a virgin.

"Mr. Bromberg," I said patiently, "Robert Swann is probably the most glamorous man in East Hampton. Women are crazy about him—all but Nicole, that is—so why should he notice me? I'm fat, Mr. Bromberg. Fat."

"But you are also beautiful," said Arnold. "Beautiful, and sensitive, and amusing. I cannot tell you what cheer you have brought to my life."

"Cheer?"

"Every day of the week, Miss Formica, at a quarter to twelve, I realize that you are coming to work and my heart lifts. You cheer my humble house."

Mr. Bromberg, I wanted to say, I may cheer your humble house, but that is not the same as being passionately desired by Robert Swann. Not at all the same as being kissed by a man who looks like a Greek god. "Well," I said lamely. "Thank you."

There was nothing more to discuss. Arnold Bromberg seemed uncomfortable, and I—realizing that we were still calling each other Mister and Miss—felt uncomfortable too. I had a sudden image of Arnold and me growing old together, calling each other Mr. Bromberg and Miss Formica. Then, surprising me, he asked, "What do you want to do with your life? After college, I mean."

"Gee," I said. "I don't know. I'm not sure."

"What is your fondest dream? If you could have anything in the world, besides Mr. Swann, of course, what would it be?"

"To be a writer," I said.

We stared at each other. Because I was just as surprised as he was. A writer? Where had the words come from?

"But how marvelous!" said Arnold Bromberg. "What kind of writing?"

"Fiction," I said. "Short stories and novels. Plays, maybe. And poems."

"Yes, yes, I can see the whole thing," Arnold said with excitement. "Fiction writing would suit you."

"It would?" I said, more amazed than ever.

"Of course it would! You have the temperament of a writer, Miss Formica, I'm sure of it. Who is your favorite author?"

"Isak Dinesen," I said. Because I had just seen the movie *Out of Africa* and then rushed to a bookstore and bought all of her books.

"Mine too!" Arnold exclaimed. "Isn't that a coincidence?"

And then an egret flew by.

It was definitely an egret, a big white one with a long neck and black legs. The trouble was that Arnold and I got so excited that we didn't have time to see it properly. Arnold dropped the binoculars, then I tried to grab them, then we *both* tried to grab them—and by that time, the egret was gone. "Damn," I said. "Was that an egret?"

Arnold laughed. "It was indeed, and we missed it. But I told you an egret would fly by, and it did. All one needs is a little faith, Miss Formica, and the universe unfolds. Mysteries. Mysteries at our very fingertips."

After a while we walked back to town, me thinking about Robert, and Arnold probably thinking about egrets. The humidity was terrible, and I was looking forward to going home and having a cool shower. As we entered Sag Harbor and began to stroll up the main street, I thought of something. "Did you ever locate that organ? You know. The one you were looking for."

Arnold shook his head. "I'm sorry to say that I did not. All I need is a small electric organ on which to practice, but they don't seem to exist around here. On a rental basis, that is."

We were walking up Madison Street now, just a block from the Whalers Church, and so the idea came quite naturally. "Why don't you practice in a church?" I said. "I'm sure people wouldn't mind."

Arnold Bromberg and I looked at each other. Then we headed for the Whalers Church—which is a huge, beautiful old building in a style that used to be called Egyptian Revival. It is one of the landmarks of Sag Harbor, but it doesn't have a steeple because the steeple blew down in a hurricane and nobody bothered to put it on again. But the church is still imposing—big and white and square.

The front doors were open, so Arnold and I mounted the steps. "Nobody's around," I said. "And there's a pipe organ up on the balcony."

"Do you think I should?" whispered Arnold.

"Sure. Go upstairs and play something. I'll be the audience."

Arnold disappeared for a moment, and I could hear his footsteps on the creaky back stairs. I had never been alone in this church before, and so I studied it carefully. Very conservative and plain, with pale sea-green walls and polished wood. Very stark and interesting. Arnold emerged on the balcony and waved. I waved back, wondering if he really knew how to play something as complicated as an organ.

He sat down at the keyboard and studied it. He looked small and far away, and I saw that he was fiddling with the organ's knobs. First he pulled out one, and then another, until he was satisfied. Then he bowed his head and paused for a moment. He began to play.

I had closed my eyes, afraid that some awful sound would come out of the organ, and afraid that Arnold was about to make a fool of himself. But I needn't have worried—because what came out of that organ was the most fantastic music I had ever heard. It was like Bach himself was playing. Or maybe Handel. Music absolutely *poured* out of the instrument, filling the entire church, swelling and building and climbing up through the air like liquid gold. And Arnold was the cause of it all.

He played and played. Stuff that sounded like Bach, and many pieces I had never heard before. Church music, religious music, hymns. And I was so astonished by the whole thing that for the second time that day my eyes filled with tears. What was life all about, when an oddball like Arnold Bromberg could play such magnificent music while Robert and Nicole were watching polo? What was the meaning of the whole damn thing when people were so separate and so lonely? And as the music swelled louder, and as I thought of Robert and how much I loved him, I put my head down on the pew in front of me and wept.

14

MARSHA STRAWBERRY was talking about identity. It was my third session with her, and she was talking about

91

identity and sex-role stereotyping. I kept nodding off and falling asleep as she spoke, but I couldn't help it. I had been having insomnia.

"Getting fat is really a feminist act," said Miss Strawberry. "It is a challenge to sex-role stereotyping and our concept of womanhood."

"Right," I said, stifling a yawn. "Absolutely."

"While becoming fat does not change the roots of sexual oppression, an examination of the *causes* that lead women to eat compulsively can help us to . . ."

She had lost me, because first of all I was sleepy, and second of all I had other things to think about besides the roots of sexual oppression. What I wanted to think about was Robert, and the date that he, Nicole and I had had a few nights ago. It was the first time that they had included me in one of their evenings—and I had been so excited about it that I had almost made myself sick. I had returned to my diet at once, gone to the beauty parlor and had my hair streaked blond, gone to Shirlee's Dress Shop and purchased a tentlike dress that was, nevertheless, sort of pretty. Blue cotton with long sleeves. I had borrowed a pair of my mother's high heels, white leather, and she had also loaned me a white leather purse. At the last moment I had put on a strand of pearls, and then, boarding the bus, had set out to meet Robert and Nicole at a Chinese restaurant in Southampton. My mother had been startled by all this activity, but of course I hadn't told her the truth. I mean, I could hardly say that I was going out on a date with a couple, so I had said that a boy from school was taking me to the movies. Poor old Mom had been thrilled, and Daddy had given me a broad wink as I left the house that night. "Be a good girl," he said. "But have fun."

Robert and Nicole were already seated in the restaurant when I arrived, and while Nicole looked happy to see me, Robert did not. In fact, he looked annoyed as I sat down at the table. "Hi," he said glumly. "How are you?" I could tell that he was not thrilled by my presence, but nevertheless he had spoken. The most recent words that Robert had said to me were, "Would you hand me a towel?" but now he had said, "Hi. How are you?" It was a beginning.

A pause here, to explain that Robert and Nicole had been dating for three weeks now, and that Nicole wanted to put an end to the whole thing. She only saw Norman the bullfighter on weekends, but she still felt disloyal to him—and, as she kept telling me, Robert was boring. On the other hand, she had gone to dinner at his house and met his family. Robert's grandmother had been a concert singer in Europe and still kept an apartment in Paris. Robert's mother was a kind of sportswoman who had once raised Irish setters. Robert's father, said Nicole, was as boring as Robert. But she did like the grand-mother. "She has the style of a European woman," said Nicole. "She has class."

We all ordered soft drinks and, as I realized that this was the first time I had ever been out in the world with Robert Swann, a chill went down my spine. He was wearing gray slacks made of some very lightweight material, and a gray-and-burgundy madras shirt. A gray cashmere sweater was thrown over his shoulders, in case it got chilly. He looked so beautiful, so perfect, that I could have cried. Nicole looked good too, but then she always did. A striped cotton dress belted tightly in the middle. Very high heels. Lots of jewelry.

As the first course—egg rolls—arrived, Robert began to talk about cars. Ignoring me as usual, he began to tell Nicole about the first car he had ever owned, a dark-blue Citroën. "It was really an interesting car," he said. "Got it in Europe one summer when Mom and I went over to visit Grandy. You've driven in Citroëns, haven't you?"

Nicole sighed. "But of course, Robert. I am French. And the Citroën is also French."

"It has air-oil suspension," Robert said. "It's really interesting."

Air-oil suspension, I thought. That's what I need.

Nicole switched topics. From air-oil suspension she detoured into a little series of stories about *me*—all of them untrue, of course, but I guess she wanted to turn the spotlight on me for a change. "This girl," she was saying, "this Skylar, she put you and me to shame, Robert. Our friend Skylar here is an adventuress."

Adventuress? What was she leading up to? Robert's mind, obviously, was still on Citroëns and he was eating his egg roll. I glanced at a mirror across the room and saw myself—a hippo wearing a blue cotton dress. I had thought I looked pretty, but I didn't. I looked like a hippo.

"Yes," Nicole said, "this child is an adventuress. She not only go to Switzerland to ski, she get involved in a spy ring there. In Zürich."

God! I thought. What are you doing, Nicole?

Robert looked up from his egg roll. "What?"

"A spy ring," I echoed. Because there was nothing else to do. If Nicole said I was a spy, then I would become a spy. In Switzerland.

Robert looked at me suspiciously. "You've been to Switzerland?"

"Uh, yes," I said. "To ski and all that. I'm very much into skiing."

"Whereabouts in Switzerland?"

"Davos!" Nicole cried. "She ski in Davos every year, don't you, Skylar? And then, down in Zürich, she get involved with a spy ring. All by accident, of course, but very dangerous."

"It was a *small* spy ring," I said to Robert.

The main course arrived—lobster and chicken dishes for the two of them, and duckling with vegetables for me. The waiter poured us cups of hot tea. Nicole passed around little plates of sweet and sour sauce.

I am not exactly a genius, but even I knew that I did not have the figure of a skier. Why had Nicole said skiing? I was too fat to ski.

It was obvious that Robert hadn't bought the story of me and the spy ring, but he was glancing at me from time to time as he ate. "What kind of skis do you use?" he asked.

"Uh . . . Bromberg skis," I said. "They're made in Germany."

"Never heard of them."

"Oh, but yes," said Nicole. "The Bromberg ski, it is internationally famous."

We finished the main course and ordered dessert. Kumquats and fortune cookies. Robert was looking restless and Nicole was looking bored. As for me, I just kept glancing at that mirror across the room. Why had I thought I looked nice? I looked like a hippo with its hair streaked blond. A hippo wearing pearls.

We ate our kumquats and opened our fortune cookies. Robert's cookie said, "He who hesitates is lost," and Nicole's said, "Wisdom and beauty are rarely bedfellows." As for my fortune cookie, it announced to all the world, "He who stuffs himself has a fool for an appetite."

"Well," said Nicole.

"Well," said Robert.

"Well," I said. "That was a nice meal."

Robert took some bills out of his pocket and handed them to the waiter. The waiter brought the change. The three of us sat there for a moment. It was obvious that Robert wanted to have the rest of the evening alone with Nicole—but he didn't know what to do about it. As for Nicole, she looked comatose. Bored, I could hear her saying silently to herself. I am bored, bored, bored.

"Let's go outside and get some air," Robert suggested. And that's when the accident occurred.

Are you ready for this? We headed for the revolving door, and Nicole got into the first compartment and revolved her way out onto the sidewalk. Robert got into the second compartment, and I—without thinking—pushed in with him. It was one of the stupidest things I have ever done in my life, and even thinking about it makes me ill, but I lost my head and squeezed into this tiny compartment with Robert Swann. Upon which we got stuck. I mean, those compartments are very narrow, and made for just one person, so that the combination of Robert and me was a disaster. For some reason, the revolving door stopped revolving. Nicole called for help.

I had always wanted to be close to Robert, but not

in this way. We were stuck together, glued together, both of us perspiring heavily as the restaurant manager tried to get the door to revolve again. But it wouldn't. I had mucked up the works of the goddam thing, and eventually they had to phone for a mechanic. Robert had gone beet red, he was so angry, and I was beginning to think that I might be sick all over his madras shirt. Duckling and vegetables. Kumquats. "I'm so sorry," I kept saying. "I'm so sorry about this." But he was not appeased. "What have you *done*?" he said to me. "Why did you *do* that?"

It took thirty minutes to get the two of us out of that compartment—thirty minutes of me sweating and trying not to be sick, and thirty minutes of Robert saying over and over, "Why did you *do* that?" but eventually the mechanic got us out onto the street. By now we had drawn a crowd, and people applauded as we got sprung. The trouble is that just as we erupted onto the sidewalk, I tripped and fell flat on my face. "I've hurt my ankle!" I said to Nicole. "Oh, God. I think I've broken it."

The manager, his eyes swimming with visions of lawsuits, went back into the restaurant and phoned an ambulance. And before I knew it, I was being whisked away to Hampton Hospital, the sirens going full blast. Robert and Nicole followed behind in Robert's car—and that's how we spent the rest of the evening. In the emergency room. Or rather, in the waiting room of the emergency room. Because there were a lot of people ahead of us. Children with bloody noses, a man with a broken arm, babies who wouldn't stop screaming, old people who looked like they were already dead. By the time the emergency room doctor took me, two hours had passed, and Robert did not just look angry. He looked wild. Oblivious to his rage, Nicole kept saying, "Poor baby, poor little Skylar. She twist the ankle. She hurt herself."

To make a long story short, it was not broken, only sprained. But by now, it was eleven o'clock. Robert drove me home—he and Nicole in the front seat, me in the back—and without saying a word he helped me out onto the sidewalk in front of my house. I expected him to say *something*, some few words of sympathy, but he was too angry. For one moment I hated him, and then I took the hatred back. Why shouldn't he have been angry? I had ruined the evening for all of us.

"In overfeeding yourself," Miss Strawberry was saying, "you are trying to reject your mother's role, while at the same time reproaching your mother. Do you see what I'm aiming at, Skylar? Do you get the point?"

"Uh, yes, Miss Doctor," I said. "I mean, Doctor Marsha. I get it."

Marsha Strawberry sighed. "I don't feel that you've

99

been listening to me. I feel that your mind is elsewhere."

"Not at all," I replied. "It's just that I have this sprained ankle and it hurts."

"How much have you lost this week?"

"Three pounds," I lied. "Three and a half, maybe."

"Do you take any form of exercise?"

"Yes," I said. "Bicycling."

The word "bicycling" brought Arnold Bromberg to mind—brought him to mind as sharply as if he had been in the room. I thought of his failing cheesecake business and his bicycle. I thought of him saying, down by the pond, that I was beautiful and sensitive. Wouldn't you know that it would be someone like Arnold who would say such words to me? Not the Robert Swanns of this world, not the gorgeous people, but the Arnold Brombergs.

Miss Strawberry was handing me a pad and a pencil. "Let's try something," she said. "Just a little experiment. Draw yourself for me."

"Draw myself? But I can't draw."

"That doesn't matter. Just make some image on this pad, some image that you feel looks like you."

I stared at the blank piece of paper. "Well," I said, "OK."

What I had intended to draw was a stick figure with a round belly and a big head. You know. The kind that children in kindergarten make. But that's not what came out, not exactly. I finished the drawing and handed it over.

"But this is a bug!" said Miss Strawberry. "Did you mean to draw a bug?"

I took the drawing back from her. "I wasn't aware that it was a bug. But you're right."

"You have drawn yourself as a fat bug," Miss Strawberry said, obviously pleased. "An insect. Something lowly and something that can be squashed. Bugs have many connotations, Skylar. Bugs were often mentioned by Freud."

So were a lot of other things, I thought, but I didn't say this to her. Instead, feeling more tired than I had ever felt in my life, I said, "OK, Mrs. Strawberry. Let's talk about bugs."

15

I HAD GAINED another four pounds. How? By eating pancakes with bacon, hot-fudge sundaes and cashew nuts. By consuming whole Pepperidge Farm cakes in the parking lot of the supermarket. By feasting on tuna melt sandwiches and chocolate malts. I was eating more crazily than I had ever eaten in my life, attributing it all, of course, to that disastrous night at the Chinese restaurant. Rita Formica was killing Skylar Cunningham—not with bullets, not with bombs, but with food.

Let me explain something to you. Skylar Cunningham was all the women I had ever known and envied. Starting with Lana Turner in old movies, and going all the way up to my mother, Skylar Cunningham was the personification of Miss America. She was skinny and sexy and cute. She was bright, but not too bright, because too much intelligence scares the boys. She was a terrific wife and mother, but always passionate in bed. She cooked like a chef, but in a low-cut dress. She was my mother—holding down a job, running a household, having hobbies and *still* looking terrific—and she was also Jane Fonda and Nancy Reagan and Raquel Welch. She was homebody and career woman, perfect mother and perfect lay—and she never, ever, got fat.

Who was Rita then? Rita was Bella Abzug and Tugboat Annie and Calamity Jane. Rita was me in my crummy overalls and straw hat, and the lady with varicose veins carrying a shopping bag down the street. Rita was old women who find themselves going bald, obese teenagers with pimples, the fat lady in the circus. Rita was not really American. She was an outlaw, a renegade—and that part made her feel pretty good. But when she sat down in a restaurant or a theater, and looked at other females, she felt a little sick. Other females had had their hair done by delicate male hairdressers and had worked for hours on their makeup. Other females were wearing bras and girdles, high heels, sexy earrings, bracelets that jangled, skintight pants, blouses that showed cleavage. How could a person be female in America and look like Rita Formica? She couldn't.

Why does it matter so much? I kept asking myself after the incident of the Chinese restaurant. Why does it *matter* how I look? I am a nice person and I am not completely stupid. Arnold Bromberg thinks that I could even be a writer someday. I get good marks in school and people like me. I am often the life of the party. I am kind to dogs.

That was the voice of Rita. The voice of Skylar, on the other hand, said this:

"You dope. No man in the world will ever want you unless you get thin, and work on your hair, and learn how to put on makeup. No man in America will ever love you if you are smarter than he is. Transform yourself, Rita! Get those pounds off, start jogging and jumping rope, tone up that flabby flesh with yoga and massage. Swim, Rita, swim! Read all the self-help books and learn to please your man. Subscribe to *Cosmopolitan* magazine and become orgasmic. Greet your man at the door each night dressed as a cowgirl or a cocktail waitress. Use a foreign accent and ask him to make love to you on the kitchen floor. Get with it, Rita, or you will be alone forever."

This was the conflict I was going through and those were the voices that I heard. And even though I went to the club with Nicole every day, I withdrew whenever she and Robert were together. Nicole said that by now he had forgotten the incident of the Chinese restaurant, but *I* had not forgotten. I was still embarrassed and miserable, and one night I even phoned Arnold Bromberg and told him the whole story. And do you know what Arnold did? He went over to his bookshelf, took out a copy of Shakespeare, and read *Hamlet* to me for two hours. Arnold saw that I was in the middle of a conflict, able to move neither this way nor that, and Hamlet had been in the same fix. He read Shakespeare beautifully, if I do say so, and believe me, Shakespeare is not my idea of jolly entertainment. "To be or not to be!" Arnold breathed into the telephone. "*That* is the question."

Then, exactly one week after the incident of the Chinese restaurant, my whole world fell apart.

16

IT BEGAN WITH A phone call from Nicole at six in the morning—and to understand Nicole, you have to realize that she never rises before ten. Her need to sleep is so intense that she had cut down her hours at the Heavenly to just four a day. Sleep made her beautiful, she said. Sleep was her restorative.

So. There I was in bed, having had insomnia all night, when the phone rang. And from the moment Nicole said, "Mouse?" I knew that something was wrong. Her voice was hoarse and strained. "I need to see you, my mouse," she said tensely. "We must talk."

It was Wednesday, her day off, so she picked me up in her old blue Toyota and we went to the beach. Nicole has a beach sticker on her car, so we drove to Bridge-hampton, parked, and began to walk along near the surf. It was only eight o'clock and there weren't many people around. The thing was, Nicole could not seem to get to the point. She talked about me and my diet—or lack of it—and she talked about the club, but it was obvious that she was avoiding something. Finally, when we were sitting on the cool sand, staring out at the Atlantic, she said, "Mouse, darling. Something has happened."

"Oh?" I said. "No kidding. What?"

She took my hand, and to my amazement I saw that she was very upset. She looked beautiful, as always, wearing very short shorts and a white sweatshirt that said "Hampton Health and Racquet Club." But there were tears in her eyes.

"To tell you this," she began, "make me feel like the

rat of all time. Yes, mouse, I feel like a rat. But because I love you, I tell you right away. Robert and I, we sleep together. We make love."

There are moments in life when speech is not possible—and this, for me, was one of them. I just looked at her.

She ran one hand through her hair and took out a cigaret. She seemed distraught. "I have no excuse," she said, "I have no reason. It simply *happen*. We sleep together."

I had thought that my voice was gone. Indeed, I had thought that some terrible stroke of fate had rendered me voiceless forever. But it came back, and when I did speak, I sounded calm. "Why don't you tell me about it?"

"OK, OK," said Nicole nervously, "I tell you the whole thing. Because, believe me, this is not planned. It is the last thing I think of. But what I discover about Robert is that there is no other way to *relate* to him. We talk—it is boring. We go to the restaurant—it is boring. The movies—boring. But in the sack, he is not boring at all. In the sack, he is a little Mozart."

"In other words, you were trying to avoid boredom," I said.

"Exactly! It is the only thing we do so far that is not boring. Lovemaking is Robert's real hobby. Not the sport, not the workout, but the love. However, he keep running out of women the way you and me run out of Kleenex." She sighed. "Some men, they are like that."

I looked at her coldly. "What about Norman?"

Nicole put her cigaret out in the sand. *"Norman."* she said. *"Norman.* Why do you ask me about Norman? He fly to Spain, to practice the bullfighting, without even telling me! He go for two weeks without even inviting me along. Norman is the rat of all time. I never speak to him again."

I still felt calm—planning my strategy, plotting my future. "In other words," I said, "Norman and you are finished."

"Exactly. He can be gored by the bull for all I care. He can go to hell."

Don't ask me why, but I felt on top of the whole thing. The fact that I was staring at the waves and planning my death at sea is not the point here. The point is that I was calm. "So," I said at last, "what will the outcome be?"

Nicole groaned. "How do I know, little mouse? I do not plan this thing, it simply happen. I get it out of my system in a few weeks. A month, maybe."

"Do you love each other?" I asked. It had taken me ten minutes to articulate this question.

Nicole looked disgusted. "Oh chérie, you are so naive. It is not a question of love, it is a question of *lovemaking*. And they are different things."

That one hit me hard. Because—moron that I am—
I had always thought of love and sex together. Very
old-fashioned, I admit, but that's how my thinking went.
But it made the whole situation worse. If they had fallen
in love, I wouldn't have minded so much. But they had
simply fallen in sex.

Nicole stretched out on the sand and put her face up
to the sun. It was late July and she had a good tan. Her
long, thin legs were tan, and her slender arms, and her
perfect face with its straight, classic nose. I stared at the
ocean and planned my death by drowning. What you
do, said Rita Formica, is take some sleeping pills and
then swim out as far as you can. So far that you know
you'll never get back. . . . Revolting, said Skylar Cunningham, and very messy. Eventually, my dear, you
wash up on some beach all bloated and white. And *that's*
when they take your picture for the newspaper.

17

I WAS DRIVING OVER TO Wainscott in a pickup truck with
Arnold Bromberg, but my mind was on Robert Swann.
It had occurred to me that if I could only understand
Robert more deeply, more profoundly, that then I might

have a chance. Oh, I knew that he and Nicole were sleeping together at every available moment—but I also knew that passion is a fleeting thing and that sooner or later they would get tired. That, at least, is what all the self-help books on love, sex and marriage said. Passion did not last. Love did.

What did it indicate about Robert Swann that he needed constant sex? That he was insecure. And what did it indicate about him that he had chosen someone as aggressive as Nicole? Again, insecurity. No matter that he came from a rich family and had a stockbroker for a father. No matter that his grandmother had sung in Europe. Robert Swann was probably as insecure as I was, and this was now part of my strategy. Let him and Nicole exhaust themselves with passion, yes, let them wear out several mattresses. *I* would be waiting for Robert when the whole thing was over. Me—steady, dependable and kind.

As visions of Robert and Nicole in bed passed before my eyes, I stifled a sob and turned to look at Arnold Bromberg. He seemed happy, driving the borrowed pickup truck along Route 27. We were going to Wainscott to meet Daisy, his goat. It was a Sunday morning and Arnold was content.

Was Nicole really passionate, I wondered? Was Robert competent? No, no, I said to myself, this way madness lies. It was a quote from Shakespeare.

"I am so thrilled to be spending this day with you, Miss Formica," said Arnold Bromberg. "It is so wonderful of you to keep me company."

"Think nothing of it," I replied. I didn't sound enthusiastic, but I couldn't help it.

"Daisy lives with a family named Jones. They have a lovely farm, and she's happy there, I think, but I miss her."

"Yeah, you must," I said absently. Because my mind was still on Robert and Nicole. Where did they make love? At his house, or hers? Hers, of course. The Swann family would not tolerate an affair under its very roof.

"Daisy's still a very young goat," Arnold was saying. "The Joneses haven't bred her yet. They're waiting for the right mate."

So am I, I thought. Oh God, so am I. Was Nicole on the Pill? When had she lost her virginity? At the age of ten probably. At the age of two.

"We're almost there," said Arnold, turning the pickup truck onto a country road. On either side of us there were fields of corn. A mile away was the ocean. I glanced at Arnold Bromberg. He was wearing a clean but shabby summer suit and a brown tie. No one wears a tie in the Hamptons, especially in summer, but I figured that Arnold had dressed up for Daisy. Weird, I thought. Some men visit their divorced wives and children on Sundays. Arnold visits his goat.

Another thing about Arnold is that he was wearing sneakers. He seemed to wear them all the time, with business suits as well as blue jeans, and I found this very odd. In an age of jogging shoes, Arnold wore sneakers. Clean ones, always. White.

We were turning onto a dirt path and in the distance was a farm. Quite a big one, with outbuildings and a silo and all that. One of the things about the Hamptons is that it is farm country and resort country all at once. A nice combination.

"There she is!" said Arnold excitedly, as he parked the truck. "Over there, in that field."

A woman standing outside one of the buildings waved to us, and we waved back. Then Arnold and I walked across the field to meet Daisy. She was tethered on a long rope under a tree.

I don't know what I expected of Daisy, but I have to admit that I was disappointed. I mean, she was only a goat. Clean enough, but not too bright.

To my amazement, Arnold Bromberg got down on his knees and embraced her. "Here's my girl," he said. "Here's my sweetheart."

I was very surprised. Because I had never seen Arnold like this before. He actually kissed Daisy on the forehead. "It's my baby," he said to her. "It's my own sweet girl."

The goat didn't seem impressed. She just stood there

chewing on something and looking bored as Arnold petted her and talked baby talk to her. I couldn't see anything unusual about her, but you never know.

Arnold reached into his pocket and took out a sandwich that was wrapped in wax paper. "She loves cheese sandwiches," he explained. "I always bring her one."

Daisy ate her sandwich as Arnold watched approvingly. Then the three of us sat down together in the field. Arnold and I sat cross-legged. Daisy folded all four legs under herself and sank to the ground. "Such a sweet girl," Arnold was saying. "Such a brave sweet girl."

I studied Arnold Bromberg. There was something sad about him lavishing all his affection on a goat when, actually, he could have made someone a very nice husband. He was talented, too. I mean, there was probably no one in Long Island, if not New York State, who could play the organ the way he did. I wasn't a connoisseur of this instrument, but I felt I was right all the same. "Mr. Bromberg?" I said.

He turned his attention from Daisy to me. "Yes, Rita? I mean Miss Formica." His eyes looked very green in the summer light. Sea green.

"What was the last piece you played for me that day? You know. The day you played in the church."

Arnold thought for a moment. "I'm not sure. . . . I

think it was the Toccata in D Minor, the 'Dorian Toccata and Fugue.' Yes, that's what it was."

"I really liked that piece. I can still hear it."

"How nice of you to say so. It dates from the period of Bach's life in Weimar, where his chief duties were as organist."

"You're certainly well informed," I said. "About Bach, I mean. How's your book coming along?"

"Well, thank you, very well. I've done a hundred pages. Miss Formica?"

"Yes?" I said, looking at Daisy, who was sleeping now, her head nodding onto her chest. "Yes, Mr. Bromberg?"

"If you don't mind my asking, how have you been these past days? Emotionally, I mean."

I didn't mind his asking—because who else in the world gave a damn how I felt? Nobody. "I don't mind your asking at all," I replied. "And if you want to know the truth, emotionally I have not been too great. Emotionally, as a matter of fact, I have been a basket case."

His face fell. "I'm so sorry. Is it the situation with Mr. Swann?"

For the second time that day, I stifled a sob. And then I proceeded to tell him what had happened between Robert and Nicole—proceeded to tell Arnold Bromberg that my best friend was sleeping with the man I loved.

I knew I was taking a chance. Because Arnold Bromberg was very virginal. He wasn't just a minister's son, he was a *minister*—pure, chaste, unworldly, kind. He played the organ. He was writing a book on Bach. He quoted Shakespeare.

Nevertheless. As Daisy began to snore, I told Arnold everything that had happened. I did not mince words and I did not bowdlerize my story. Nicole Sicard was making love to Robert Swann at every possible opportunity. On beds and couches and in easy chairs. In her bathtub and her kitchen. Bathtubs, she had once told me, were sexy.

I watched Arnold's face as I told him this tale, waiting for the moment when shock would overwhelm him. But Arnold surprised me. "What a distressing story," he said. "But psychologically, quite interesting."

"You find it interesting, Mr. Bromberg? Psychologically?"

Arnold took out a clean white handkerchief and wiped his brow. The day was growing warmer. "I do indeed. First of all, Miss Formica, I can understand how the situation must make you feel."

"Like hell."

"Yes," he echoed, "like hell. Because there is nothing so painful as unrequited love. But psychologically, the situation is worth looking at. I mean, what do you think is motivating your friend Nicole?"

"Lust," I said.

Arnold nodded. "That's always possible, but lust is not a mindless thing, and since you tell me that this woman is your friend, why do you think she is doing this to you?"

He had me stumped. Why *was* Nicole sleeping with Robert when she knew I loved him? That was the question.

"Does friendship preclude lust?" I asked Arnold. God! I thought. I am beginning to sound just like him.

"Yes," he said, "it does. Friendship is sacred, and one of the most important things in this world. It most definitely precludes lust."

"Well, then maybe she's not the friend I thought she was."

"That is a definite possibility," said Arnold Bromberg.

We looked at each other—a long, honest look. A look that I couldn't have had with anyone else. Because it was beginning to occur to me that Arnold was a very straight person. I don't mean straight as opposed to gay or anything. I mean direct, honest, trustworthy.

"Daisy's asleep," I said after a minute.

"I know. It's the weather. Hot weather always affects her."

"Maybe you'll take her back someday. When you have your own home."

A sad expression crossed Arnold's face, but I didn't know the reason for it. "Are you going to make cheese-cakes tonight?" I asked.

He stared across the cornfields. "I don't know. Business has been so slow these past weeks . . . I just don't know."

I wanted to make him feel better, so I said, "Arnold? I mean Mr. Bromberg. Would you quote a little Shake-speare for me? Some *Hamlet* or something?"

He looked surprised. "Do you like Shakespeare?"

"No," I confessed, "I don't. But I like your voice."

"Very well, then. I'll quote you some T. S. Eliot.

> *"For most of us, there is only the unattended*
> *Moment, the moment in and out of time,*
> *The distraction fit, lost in a shaft of sunlight,*
> *The wild thyme unseen, or the winter lightning*
> *Or the waterfall, or music heard so deeply*
> *That it is not heard at all, but you are the music*
> *While the music lasts. . . ."*

"That's beautiful," I said. "Is there any more?"

"There is. But I can't remember it."

"Do you like T. S. Eliot a lot?"

"Yes. He means everything to me."

Arnold was looking away from me, over the fields and toward the ocean. And suddenly I wanted to tell him how dry his cheesecake was. I wanted to tell him to get out of the cheesecake business entirely and go into something more profitable. I wanted to tell him how intelligent he was—much too intelligent to be running a cheesecake business—and I also wanted to tell him that I admired him. But do you know something? I didn't say any of that, not a single word. And as we drove back to Sag Harbor in the borrowed pickup truck, I felt more depressed than ever.

18

IT WAS TWO DAYS LATER, and I was sitting in Marsha Strawberry's dark little office reading my stream-of-consciousness diary to her. Miss Strawberry looked pained as I read aloud, but what the hell. She had asked me to do stream of consciousness, and I had done it. This is how the excerpt went.

> Robert reminds me of a white cake with vanilla icing, a cake both pure and sexual. Arnold, on the other hand, reminds me of a deep and mysterious red wine. Don't like wine. Don't drink at all, but maybe I should. Arnold is a deep red wine served at a medieval banquet. Robert is the best birthday

cake in the world. Did Mom ever give me birthday parties when I was little? Yes, but I never liked them. Oh shit, it's too confusing. What is Nicole like? Like a passionate omelet, one that's made with mushrooms and cheese. So here we have vanilla cake and an omelet and red wine. Ugh. Oh God, oh God, I'm so hungry today. All I can think of is donuts.

Marsha Strawberry looked stunned. She was wearing a sleeveless dress, and stockings and heels. A neat haircut, a faint trace of lipstick. She looked perfect, but embalmed. When I finished reading she took off her glasses and stared at me. "I find that entry very vulgar," she said. "Very vulgar indeed."

I closed the diary. It made a snapping sound. "Well, I'm sorry, Mrs. Marsha. I mean Dr. Strawberry. But you did ask me to do stream of consciousness."

"I did not, however, ask for vulgarity. The vulgarity was unnecessary."

"But that's like censoring a dream! I mean, it was my unconscious speaking—not me."

Miss Strawberry sighed. And I saw how discouraged she felt about me. She wasn't a bad dame, really, just repressed. I decided to tell her the truth about my eating.

"I've been eating," I said. "For many weeks. Like a maniac."

She went visibly pale. "You have?"

"Yes. I have."

"But why didn't you tell me! Why did you pretend?"

"I don't know," I said. "Well yes, I do know. I've been very upset about something, and it's been driving me to eat. Donuts in particular."

A cold look came over Marsha Strawberry's face. "A normal person does not combine donuts and grief," she said. "A normal person uses a Band-Aid for a wound, not a potato chip."

"I never said I was normal," I said quietly. "If I was normal, I wouldn't be here. Look, Madam Strawberry—I mean, Mrs. Strawberry—I'm eating my way through the Hamptons and I need your help."

"I am really very shocked that you lied to me, Skylar. I thought we were making progress."

"We have been," I said. "I mean, I've learned a lot from you. It's just that I'm bingeing and can't seem to stop."

"Have you no control?" Miss Strawberry said angrily. "Have you no self-discipline?"

"*What?*"

"Have you no way of controlling that disgusting appetite of yours? Western civilization is founded on the ideals of discipline and husbandry and control."

"What has that got to do with me, for God's sake?"

119

She threw her hands up in the air. "I simply cannot work with you! You are stubborn to a fault, and what's more, you are a liar."

Wow, I thought, I would not have believed this. But then I realized what the problem was. The problem was that Marsha Strawberry had never been hungry in her life. Not for food, or sex, or money, or for beautiful possessions. Not for travel to distant places, or adventure, or romance. She was a person without hunger, and therefore could not understand me. I rose to my feet. "Good-bye," I said. And, as Miss Strawberry's mouth dropped open in surprise, I made a graceful exit from her life.

It was four in the afternoon, and I had another hour to spend at the club before my mother picked me up. Robert and Nicole, of course, were not around. They were never at the club these days, so urgent was their passion for one another, so great their need to make love.

I went into the room where the stationary bicycles were, and mounted one. Very slowly, I began to pedal. I looked at myself in the mirror in front of me and saw a pretty, but very fat girl trying to pedal a bicycle. Fat neck, fat arms, fat legs. Huge hips. Floppy breasts. I kept on bicycling. Just because a person feels like sleeping with someone, I said to myself, should she do it? Is life based on *urges*? Arnold Bromberg says that friendship is sacred, and I think he's right. What is all this crap about Nicole not being able to control the situation? Did he drug her? Was she hypnotized?

My legs were getting tired, but I kept on pedaling. Let's be blunt, I said to myself. What Nicole is doing with Robert is what *you* do every day with food. You tell yourself that it's out of your control, that you have no choice. You tell yourself that you are the victim of your urges. But God! I mean, really! Is that true?

I kept on pedaling. It wasn't true, and I was not the victim of my urges unless I wanted to be. I DID NOT HAVE TO OVEREAT. And this idea was so exciting that I pedaled even harder. This goddam thing of food and loneliness and sex and emotional starvation was completely within my control. I did not have to be the fat lady in the circus. I did not have to be a freak. "You are only sixteen!" said the voice of Rita Formica. Because, for the moment, Skylar Cunningham had vanished.

19

I WAS NOT OVEREATING. I wasn't dieting, but neither was I overeating. And the experience was so new and strange that I kept the whole thing to myself. I didn't want to talk about it. I just wanted to see what would happen. I wasn't dieting, but I wasn't bingeing either. I was like a tightrope walker. Balancing.

The summer was almost over, and what had I done with it? Nothing but suffer over Robert Swann. Nothing but show up at Arnold's every day, where there was no work to be done and no cheesecake to deliver. But I went to the club now for *me*, not anyone else, and I swam there, and rode the bicycles, and took aerobics. I did not care that the people around me were thin, and I did not care that a few of them glanced at me with pity. In some strange way I didn't care about anything. I was not overeating and I was not gorging myself— and that's all that mattered.

Nicole had quit her job in order to spend every moment with Robert, so I saw very little of her. And when I did see her, our conversations were strained. As for Robert, I knew that I still loved him—that I might always love him—but it was becoming harder and harder to kid myself. Robert cared about Nicole, not me. It was possible that he did not write poetry at night.

Sometimes I would see Robert and Nicole on the streets of East Hampton, and the three of us would stop and chat, and everything would seem perfectly nice. But they looked different these days. Like they were engaged in a conspiracy or something—like they had a plot. They held hands constantly. They finished each other's sentences. They were nervous. But the thing that was offensive to me was that they had begun to dress alike. The same kind of sweat suits, the same jogging shoes. Nicole had embraced fitness with a vengeance and had bought herself a whole wardrobe of workout clothes. The only thing left to happen, I decided, was for Robert to start speaking French.

Another thing that annoyed me was the way Nicole was calling Robert "Ro-Bear." He had once been "Robert," English pronunciation only, but now he was "Ro-Bear" this and "Ro-Bear" that. Don't ask me why, but it drove me wild.

Where had the summer gone? I had only been to the beach a few times. I had not been to a movie. And Arnold Bromberg had gone home to Kansas. It was only for ten days, but it's odd how his absence affected me. I would walk by the Harbor Hound Dog Grooming Parlor and realize that Arnold wasn't inside—and then I would feel very strange, like my left foot was missing. What was he doing in Topeka? I wondered. Seeing an old girlfriend? No, said my new, strong, inner voice. Arnold has no girlfriends. He is a virgin.

I would pass by the Whalers Church and think of the day that Arnold had played the organ for me. Someone would say the word "farm" and I would think of Daisy the goat. Perhaps I should visit her, I thought, in Arnold's absence. No, that was crazy. I could just see myself telling my mother that I was off to Wainscott to pay a call on a goat.

I looked up Topeka, Kansas, in the encyclopedia and learned that it was mostly famous for the Atchison, Topeka and Santa Fe Railroad. I collected Arnold's mail for him at the post office. And every day that he was gone, I thought about him. Don't ask me why. When a postcard from him arrived four days after his departure, I was oddly pleased. The only thing was, the postcard didn't show Topeka, which I would have found interesting. Instead, it was a picture of Johann Sebastian Bach. "It's lovely to be here," said Arnold Bromberg, "but I also look forward to my return. Remember, dear Miss Formica, that the universe is benevolent. Remember that right action is always taking place. Sincerely, A. Bromberg."

The universe is benevolent, I said to myself, as I wandered around Sag Harbor. Right action is taking place, I repeated, as I thought of Robert and Nicole. Like a ghost, I drifted through town, wandering in and out of the dime store, the antique shops. I didn't know what to do with myself and kept getting stabs of emotional pain. Oh God, I thought, it's over. I'll never have him, and I could have given so much to him. Love and laughter, warmth, passion, wit. I could have devoted my entire life to Robert Swann and never *looked* at another man. . . . I had an image of myself growing old alone. Someone so fat she could hardly leave the house. Someone who had to be taken around in a wheelchair. I had an image of myself living on disability insurance. My illness? Fat.

Two days before Arnold Bromberg was due to return from Kansas, I found a note from Nicole in my box at the post office. "Dearest Mouse," it said, "I need so much to speak to you. Can you meet me tomorrow at eleven in the morning? Let us meet at the club, in the room of the stationary bicycles."

It was an odd place for a meeting, I thought, but the following morning I was there—dressed in sweatpants and a T-shirt. Apprehensive and nervous, I had arrived early, and now I stood on the sidelines, watching people use the bicycles. Then Nicole breezed in, wearing a pearl-gray sweat suit and pearl-gray sneakers. Her thick hair was pulled up on top of her head with a pearl-gray ribbon. She had on very bright lipstick.

Perfunctorily, we kissed on the cheek and went to sit down on one of the benches that lined the room. I knew that this was going to be an important meeting, and was sorry we were having it in a roomful of stationary bicycles.

I saw the ring at once, of course—the diamond ring on her engagement finger—but I pretended that I didn't.

My eyes went over the diamond's hard glitter for just a second, and glanced away. As far as I was concerned, I had seen nothing.

For fifteen minutes, Nicole prevaricated. She talked about Robert and the club, Robert's car, Robert's grandmother—but could not get to the point. She talked about the weather, and a movie she had seen the other night. She talked about her wardrobe and the fact that she was thinking of having her hair cut short. On and on. Meanwhile, the stationary bicycle riders kept riding, and I stayed very quiet, very still. At last, having run out of topics, Nicole said, "Mouse dear, Robert and I, we become engaged. He give me this ring. We think of marriage."

I opened my mouth to speak, but nothing came out. Trying again, I formed my words clearly and carefully. "How nice," I said. "Congratulations."

Nicole looked sad. "This has not been an easy time for us, *chérie*. The mother, the father, they do not approve. They think I am not good enough for their son! But the grandmother, she like me very much. So I think maybe it will be OK. I think that maybe Robert and I get married."

"Well, at least you'll never be bored," I said.

"Pardon?"

"Nothing. Congratulations. And *bon voyage*."

Nicole looked even sadder. "I know how this make

126

you feel, my mouse. I have some idea of your feelings. So, in the name of friendship, I ask you to forgive me."

Forgive her? Why should I have forgiven her? I was not an early Christian, to go around forgiving people. I did not forgive her. I wished her boiled in oil.

I sat there for a moment, watching the bicycle riders, who were riding without getting anywhere at all. Just like me. Riding and riding and arriving nowhere. "I have to go," I said. "I have an appointment."

Nicole looked distressed. "But we see each other soon, my mouse, yes? We do something nice together. We repair our friendship."

"Sure," I said. "Absolutely. *Au revoir*."

Without changing into my street clothes, I left the club, stopped at a phone booth to call my mother with the news that I would be taking the bus home, that she did not have to come for me—and then I headed for the Knave of Hearts Bakery. There I purchased a dozen macaroons and proceeded to eat them on a bench near the movie house. After that, I marched into an ice cream parlor and had a hot-butterscotch sundae with whipped cream, nuts, and a cherry. Having gone through the sweets, I now decided to attack the savories, and, at The Burger Palace, had a cheeseburger with French fries and a root beer. Not wanting to throw up, I decided to take an intermission—so I boarded the bus to Sag Harbor and dozed for a while as we barreled along the turnpike.

Arriving back in my hometown, I debarked and headed for the Heavenly Cafe, where I consumed a platter of blueberry pancakes and a glass of milk. It was odd, but I did not feel full and I did not feel sick. I didn't feel anything.

I went to the dime store and bought a bag of Gummy Bears. I went to the deli across the street and purchased three cinnamon donuts. And for the rest of the afternoon, I ate my way through the town of Sag Harbor. No morsel of food was safe in my presence, no donut, cookie, or potato chip could hide from me. And yet—incredible as it sounds—I couldn't get full. It was crazy. I was eating enough food for a squadron of Green Berets, and yet I couldn't get full.

I phoned my mother to say that I would be having dinner with my friend Martha, and that we might be going to a movie. And since it was dusk now, a warm purple dusk, I strolled out onto the wharf. It was Saturday night, and there is no place quite as raucous, in summer, as Sag Harbor on the weekend. People drink a lot and cruise around in pickup trucks, and there is always loud music pouring out of the disco on Bay Street. I walked up and down the wharf, staring in shop windows. Sports clothes, souvenirs, ice cream. A record store, a hot-dog stand. And then I saw a fast-food shop that had opened just last week. *Clam-in-a-Cookie* it was called.

Clam in a cookie? Who had invented such a thing? I

wanted one passionately, and so I entered this small, smelly, fast-food shop and bought one clam in a cookie wrapped in wax paper.

I went out to the wharf, where dozens of people were milling around, found a bench near some moored yachts, and looked at my clam in a cookie. It was indeed a large, pale-gray clam baked into a huge chocolate chip cookie. The cookie was in the shape of a taco, wrapped around the clam but just allowing the pale-gray object to peek out. It was, perhaps, the most disgusting thing ever invented in the modern world, the most obscene creation known to man—and so, of course, I ate it.

Ten minutes later, kneeling under the wharf where no one could see me, I threw up—and then I fainted. I don't know how long I was unconscious, but when I woke I had only one thought in mind. To phone Arnold Bromberg. I didn't even know if he was back from Kansas, but I knew that I needed him. Trembling a little, I headed for a phone booth.

20

IT WAS ONLY NINE at night, but Arnold was asleep—having had a long flight back from Kansas, a troubled flight which involved changing planes. "I need to see you," I said weakly. "Can I come over?"

He was waiting for me on the porch as I walked toward the dog grooming parlor, and he was wearing a shabby cotton bathrobe. His hair was tousled and his feet were bare—and he looked more wonderful than anything had ever looked in my life. Feeling a little dizzy, I staggered toward him.

He put out a hand to steady me. "Miss Formica? Are you ill?" And then I collapsed in his arms. "Oh, my goodness," he said, "do come inside. Poor Miss Formica, you're ill! Do you want me to call a doctor?"

Telling him please not to call a doctor, I allowed Arnold to lead me into the house. His arm around my shoulder, he helped me to the living room, which was also the kitchen, and settled me down on the couch. He placed a pillow under my head, and even though it was a warm night, he put a cotton blanket over me. Then he laid a cool compress on my forehead. "I'll make you some tea," he said. "It will soothe you."

No one except my parents had ever pampered me that way, so I started to cry. Not dramatically, just quietly and deeply, crying for my whole life as a fat person, my whole sixteen years. Arnold Bromberg sat by my side, patting me. "Poor child," he said. "Poor little girl."

Well, of course, those words made me cry even harder.

I just couldn't stop crying, but somehow it was all right. Arnold handed me a cup of herb tea. I began to sip it, and it tasted wonderful. "How was Kansas?" I asked.

"Shh," he said. "Just drink the tea. Just rest."

I took another sip of the hot, wonderful tea. "Was it nice to be home? Was Topeka nice?"

He studied me carefully. "You're pale as a ghost, my dear. What happened to you tonight?"

I gave him a weak smile. "I was raped by a clam."

I thought this was funny, but Arnold looked alarmed. *"What?"* he said.

"Nothing," I sighed. "I've just been on an eating binge, that's all. I made myself sick. I threw up."

Arnold stroked the damp hair away from my forehead. "Poor girl. Poor lonely girl."

His kindness had such an overwhelming effect on me that I started to cry again. And then I had to rush to the bathroom, where once more I was sick. I returned to the couch and lay down.

For the next hour, I told Arnold Bromberg everything. How Robert and Nicole were getting married, and how I wanted to kill myself. I told him the entire history of my eating, and, at least twice more, I burst into tears. And all through this tirade he sat by my side, listening. He didn't interrupt and he didn't offer advice. He just listened, very very carefully.

At last I was through. At last I had said everything I

needed to say. And it was only then that Arnold spoke. "I used to be fat," he said to me. "Obese."

Like a shot, I sat up on the couch. "What?"

"Until I was eighteen years old, Miss Formica, I was a very fat person. Huge."

I looked at Arnold Bromberg. He was a big man, and very tall. But he was not fat. If anything, he was simply muscular and large. I tried to picture him fat and couldn't. "I don't believe you," I said.

He pulled a kitchen chair over to the side of the couch and sat down on it facing me. "I was the fattest person in Topeka," he said. "The fattest person, perhaps, in all of Kansas."

"God! Then how did you get thin, Mr. Bromberg? You look great now. Really."

"I changed," Arnold said. "I hit bottom, as the saying goes, and then I changed."

"How?"

"The how is not important. It's the why that matters. *Why* I ate. Why you eat now."

"Why *do* I overeat?"

"You overeat to make yourself fat," Arnold said.

"And why do I want to be fat, Mr. Bromberg?"

"To protect yourself," he replied. "To protect the fragile person within."

My heart was beginning to pound. "Go on."

"Fat is an attempt to take care of ourselves. A misguided attempt, but nonetheless a very real one. Fat is like armor."

"But why am I hungry all the time?"

"Because you are trying to take care of yourself," Arnold said patiently. "Because you are trying to maintain the armor."

I was dumbstruck. On the one hand, the whole thing seemed to be true—while on the other hand, it was almost too simple to be true. "How do I get rid of my hunger?" I asked.

"By letting go."

Letting go. The words were almost magical. Because I knew what they meant. Letting go didn't mean defeat, it meant a kind of . . . turning over of everything. Of Robert and Nicole—and food. Of my image of myself as something grotesque.

"All this is very deep," I said to Arnold Bromberg.

"But it is also simple," he replied. He looked at his watch. "It's getting late, Miss Formica. Won't your mother be concerned?"

"I'll phone her," I said. "May I sleep here tonight?"

Arnold didn't bat an eye, and the fact that he didn't seemed absolutely wonderful to me. "Of course you may sleep here. But phone your family first."

I phoned Mom and told her that I was going to spend the night at Martha Moffat's house, and since Mom is very friendly with the Moffats, she said OK. I sent a

133

swift little prayer up to heaven, asking God to prevent my mother from phoning the Moffats about anything, and then I went back to the kitchen. Arnold Bromberg was making up the couch with clean sheets. "You may sleep here, or in the bedroom," he said. "Which would you prefer?"

"Here," I said, "on the couch. It's cosy."

"Try to sleep late. I'll make you a good breakfast in the morning."

I looked at Arnold Bromberg—at his bare feet and shabby bathrobe, at his curly hair—and felt something very close to joy. "I love you, Mr. Bromberg," I said. "I just didn't know it before."

Arnold Bromberg's eyes filled with tears. "Good night," he said. And then he went into his bedroom and closed the door.

21

DID I SLEEP THAT NIGHT? I must have, because I woke feeling refreshed. But on the other hand, I felt that I had been awake for hours thinking about Arnold Bromberg. The fact that I loved him, and I had told him so, was so overwhelming that I didn't want to sleep at all. I wanted to lie there in the comforting darkness, thinking about him sleeping in the next room. I wanted to stay awake till dawn, listening to the sounds of Sag Harbor. A fire engine in the distance, a dog barking, the whistle of a train. It's an odd place, really. The only place I know of where the local radio station will broadcast live from a yard sale. The only place where, in winter, there are more dogs on the street than people. Jammed with tourists in summer, lonely and bleak by Thanksgiving. A cold gray harbor town, with icy rain pelting the streets in December and all the trees on Main Street lit with delicate white lights. And winter was coming now—a winter with Arnold Bromberg.

When I woke, sunlight was pouring through the windows and Arnold was standing by the stove, waiting for the kettle to boil. He was wearing his shabby cotton robe once again, but looked very clean and scrubbed—as though he had had a shower. "Did you sleep?" he asked. "Did you get enough rest?"

I had gotten enough rest and felt perfectly fine. But I was still wearing my sweatpants and T-shirt and felt sort of grubby. "May I have a shower?" I asked him. "And then, could you possibly loan me something to wear?"

"Of course," said Arnold formally. "Do take a shower,

135

Miss Formica, and I'll leave you some clean clothes by the door. Breakfast will be ready soon."

The shower felt wonderful, and when I emerged into Arnold's bedroom I saw that he had left the following for me: A pair of Bermuda shorts and a clean white shirt. A new pair of straw bedroom slippers. I put these clothes on, aware that they were too big—even for me—but at least they were clean.

We breakfasted together on fresh fruit, eggs and toast, and more herb tea. Sunlight was flooding the room, the bells of the Catholic church were ringing out for eight-o'clock mass, and everything seemed beautiful. The only trouble was that Arnold seemed to be on edge. He was acting more formally than he had acted all summer, and I couldn't understand it. I gazed at this huge man in his cotton bathrobe, and felt a wave of overwhelming, passionate love. "Miss Formica?" he said at last.

"Yes, Mr. Bromberg?" I replied.

"Ah, Miss Formica . . . around ten hours ago, ten and a half, to be exact, you said something that startled me very much."

"I did?"

"What you said was that you loved me. This statement has kept me awake for most of the night, because I don't know how to interpret it. Do you mean that you love me as a friend? Or perhaps, a father figure?"

I looked Arnold Bromberg squarely in the eye. "No,"
I said. "I love you as a man."

Arnold folded his napkin and placed it carefully on
the table. "I find that astonishing."

"Why?"

He looked away from me, pain in his eyes. "Because
I love you too," he said. "Passionately and deeply."

I caught my breath with surprise, and then Arnold
was kneeling by my chair. He took my face in his hands
and kissed me—and I realized that a miracle was happening. Because the kiss that Arnold was giving me was
a totally new thing. It was gentle and caring, with an
element of restraint in it, but underneath there was a
volcano raging. You have to take my word about this,
because I had been kissed many times before—all by
pimply boys who just wanted to make out with me.
But this was something different. The kiss went on and
on.

"We must stop," said Arnold, his hands buried in my
hair. "We must stop now."

But we didn't stop. We just moved onto the couch,
where our kisses got deeper and deeper. Arnold kissed
my eyelids and my hair. He kissed my throat. "Are you
a virgin?" he asked.

"Yes," I murmured. "Are you?"

"No," he said. And there we left it.

I lay down on the couch and pulled him down with me. I put his hands on my breasts. With a groan, he pulled away. "We have to stop now," he said firmly. "Just for a while, Miss Formica, please."

I giggled. "Mr. Bromberg, don't you think it's time we used first names?"

He smiled. "Yes, I suppose it is."

He rose to his feet and ran both hands through his hair. He found a pack of cigarettes and lit one. I knew how excited he was, and I felt the same way, but I also knew that we had to pause for a while. Because what was happening to us was like an earthquake or a hurricane. A force of nature. I sat up on the couch and buttoned my shirt—his shirt, actually. "Arnold," I said, making myself use his first name, "were you here last year for the hurricane? You know, the big one in September."

He sat down at the kitchen table, smoking, trying to calm himself. "Yes, I was. I loved it."

"You did? I was scared to death. Mom and I sat in the basement the whole time."

"It was wonderful," said Arnold Bromberg. "I stood on the wharf for the whole thing, my face to the wind. . . . Why do you ask me this?"

I came over to the kitchen table, and although I don't smoke, I took one of his cigarets. "Because that's how I feel about you. Overwhelmed. Swept away."

Arnold took my right hand, turned it over, and kissed the palm. "I love you," he said. "From the moment you answered that ad, from the moment I saw you, I was in love."

"Me too—but I didn't know it till last night." I sat down at the table. "Do people ever call you Arnie?"

"Never. Only Arnold."

"And how old are you?"

"Thirty-two."

"Are you independently wealthy?" I asked, because suddenly I had to know everything about him.

"Not really. I'm living on a small inheritance from my uncle."

"Is your father really a minister?"

"Of course."

"And did you like being back home?"

Arnold leaned across the table and stroked my cheek. "I liked it, but I thought of you every moment that I was there. I wanted to phone you a thousand times."

"Oh, Arnold. Why didn't you?"

"Shyness," he replied.

I came around to his side of the table and put my arms around him. "You are about as shy as a lion," I said, "or a polar bear. You *appear* to be shy, but you're like a force of nature."

We were kissing again, so passionately that my mind reeled. So passionately that the only thing left to do was to go to bed together. "Let's make love," I said to him. "In bed. Please, Mr. Bromberg."

Arnold shook his head. "Not yet," he said, "not yet."

"But *why?*"

"Because you are sixteen years old and a virgin. And because I am thirty-two and not. That's why."

I couldn't believe what I was hearing. "But that's so old-fashioned!"

Arnold went over to the stove and put the kettle on. "It may be old-fashioned, but then so am I. Do you want some more tea?"

"No," I said, "I do not want some more tea. I want to go to bed with you."

"We'll work it out," he said.

We did not go to bed that morning. What we did was go to church. That's right, the Whalers Church—me wearing Arnold's Bermuda shorts, and Arnold in a business suit and sneakers. We did not disrobe and go passionately to bed—we went to a Presbyterian church where we bowed our heads and listened to the organist play Bach. He did not play half as well as Arnold, but the music was good all the same. Then we went for brunch at The Captain's Table, which is a very fancy restaurant on Main Street. I phoned my mother from this place, saying that I was having brunch with Martha, and when I came back to the table Arnold had ordered a glass of champagne. One glass. "You're not of legal drinking age," he said, "so I thought we might share this."

He held the glass for me, as I took a sip of champagne. Then he took a sip too, and after a while we sat holding hands, staring at each other. "Your eyes are so green," I said to him, "sea green. And your hair is the color of chestnuts. I love your hair, Mr. Bromberg. I love everything about you."

We couldn't stop looking at each other. And when the waiter brought the dish I had ordered, I wasn't even hungry. All of which was incredible because I had ordered crepes suzettes, thin little pancakes covered with powdered sugar and decorated with a slice of ham. In the center of the ham was a delicate slice of pineapple— and on top of the pineapple was half a maraschino cherry. This sounds vulgar, but it wasn't. It was beautiful. And yet I wasn't hungry.

"You're not eating," said Arnold.

"I know," I said. "I'm not hungry. Maybe I'll never be hungry again."

"That, I doubt. But I do think you have reached a turning point."

"You are my turning point," I said to him. "You and you alone."

"I love you, Rita," he said, not touching his food.

"I love you too," I replied. "Arnold."

22

ARNOLD AND I went to Robert and Nicole's wedding on October 10th, and whereas you may think that this event disturbed me, it did not. To begin with, the ceremony was held in the Swanns' "autumn garden," and was color coordinated. The bride was in autumn colors, and the bridesmaids, and Robert's mother, and only the minister escaped wearing an outfit that looked like a fallen leaf. As for Robert, who was perfectly dressed as always, he looked bemused. What am I getting into? said the look on his face.

Robert, I said silently, you are still beautiful and in a funny way I still love you. But it's like loving a piece of birthday cake in comparison to a deep red wine. You're all vanilla cake and pink balloons—whereas Arnold is roast beef and potatoes and vegetables. You're beautiful, Robert, but bland—and the weird thing is that I never saw it before. What will happen when you and Nicole get tired of each other? What will happen when the kids start to appear?

I wasn't jealous! Not when the minister pronounced

them man and wife, and not even when they kissed each other—such a long passionate kiss that people got nervous. Robert and Nicole were separate from me, because what mattered was that Arnold was by my side. We made a handsome couple, me a little thinner now and wearing a pretty green dress—and Arnold looking distinguished in gray slacks and a beige jacket. It's incredible that I had never realized how handsome Arnold was, but quite a few people came over to us that day and started to talk. Andrea Fletcher, who goes to my school and who is a friend of the Swanns', even came up to me and asked who Arnold was.

Why had I been so attracted to the Swanns? I ask you this seriously. Because on the day of that wedding I did not find them attractive at all. Robert's mother kept kissing people on the cheek without really kissing them, and saying, "Darling! How lovely of you to come!" or "Don't they make a charming couple?" And Robert's father, the stockbroker, kept slapping other men on the back and calling them Old Chap. The entire scenario had all the depth and meaning of a Hallmark greeting card. But after the champagne and the toasts, and after Nicole had rushed into the house to change, and after she and Robert had put their suitcases into his car, and people were milling around, and after Nicole threw her bridal bouquet at me—and I caught it!—then, all of a sudden, I felt glad for them. They were in love and they were married now, and it was fine.

Arnold and I drove back to the dog grooming parlor in the secondhand car he had just bought, and we were very quiet, very thoughtful. Because we were both thinking of our own relationship and what the future might be. It was October now, I was back in school, and we still hadn't slept together. Oh, we made love at every possible opportunity, but it never ended in the bedroom. It ended in the kitchen—with us having a cup of tea. We loved each other, we were committed to each other, but Arnold would not take that final step.

I brought him home to dinner one night—but the results were predictable. Quite simply and plainly, my parents thought he was nuts. I had introduced him as my employer at the cheesecake shop, Mr. Bromberg, but my mom is no fool. She saw right away that Arnold and I were in love, and after a while my dad saw it too. Arnold was chatting happily about the difference between Long Island and Kansas, and how much he loved shorebirds and hurricanes, but my parents looked alarmed. *I* knew that Arnold Bromberg was a serious, intelligent, and passionate person. But alas. All *they* knew was that he was weird.

I am not yet resolved on this subject. Because Arnold Bromberg was almost abnormal in his inability to earn a living, in his penchant for daydreams, in his openness and kindness and morality. Like Abe Lincoln, he would have walked miles to return a penny to a shopkeeper, and he always helped old people across the street. No stray animal could come into his life without being rescued, and he gave much of his small income to charity. Arnold was the best human being God ever made. But that did not make him normal. He was not mechanically minded and could not fix things when they broke. He did not like sports. He did not own a television set. However. His book on Bach, parts of which I had read now, was absolutely terrific, and every time he played the organ for me I was terribly moved. The only subject on which we did not agree was whether the universe was—or was not—benevolent.

Some of the things that Arnold told me about himself amazed me. That he had almost completed a Ph.D. in English Literature. That he had been an amateur actor in Topeka, with a Shakespeare group. That he had had two passionate love affairs in his life—the most recent being with a ballet dancer called Rose. He had followed her all the way to New York, trying to get her to marry him, but she wouldn't because her career came first. My mind reeled as I tried to picture Arnold in love with a ballerina. And, quite unreasonably, I felt jealous. Was Rose pretty, I kept asking him, was she passionate? What did Rose have that I didn't? Where was Rose now?

"She's in Europe," Arnold said patiently. "Far, far away."

"So when is she coming back?" I inquired. "I want the date and the time."

He laughed. "My darling, you sound jealous."

"Jealous! I am already planning her assassination. By the corps de ballet."

Arnold wrapped his arms around me and held me tight. "It is you I love," he said. "You and you alone."

Guess what? By the day of Robert and Nicole's wedding, I had lost ten pounds. And two weeks later, I had lost fourteen. Even my mother couldn't help being impressed with this, and of course I told her that it was all because of Arnold Bromberg. Mr. Bromberg was helping me diet, I explained. Mr. Bromberg had once been fat himself.

It wasn't that Arnold's diet was different from other diets—because most diets, except the crazy ones, are about the same. So it wasn't the fact that I wasn't eating sugar, or bread, or potatoes—or Gummy Bears—it was the fact that I was succeeding at something for the first time in my life. I was letting go of my compulsion to eat. Not *controlling it*, but letting it go. Arnold, of course, said that I was doing this all by myself, but the secret is that he dieted along with me. He would add in a potato or a piece of bread for himself at every meal, and he might, when alone, have some apple pie. But we were doing it together, planning menus and counting calories, and it made all the difference in the world.

One day Arnold took me to Stern's and bought me some clothes. Just a pair of tweed slacks and two sweaters, but they were not Fat Clothes. He was like a mother hen, bustling around, holding up outfits for me to look at, showing me things I might fit into within a few months.

"How about this?" he said, standing in the middle of Ladies' Sportswear and holding up a sweater. "It goes with your eyes."

"I think I prefer yellow," I said.

"All right, all right," he said busily. "We'll take a yellow sweater to go with the brown slacks."

"Maybe the brown slacks need a *brown* sweater," I said, feeling unsure of the whole thing.

"Nonsense," Arnold replied. "Mix and match."

Which made me burst out laughing, though he couldn't understand why.

We brought Daisy the goat back to live at the dog grooming parlor. We adopted two kittens from the local animal shelter. Arnold taught me to drive the second-hand Ford he had purchased—and in the midst of everything I went to Peterson High, and did my homework, and appeased my parents. They were very conflicted. Because on the one hand, they could see that Arnold was good for me, and that he was getting me to lose weight—while on the other hand, he made them shudder. He was so different from anyone they had ever known. His values, to them, were so odd.

I persisted, and brought him home to dinner again. I persisted, and had my mom over to the dog grooming parlor for tea. I persisted, each and every day, and asked that Arnold be invited to Thanksgiving dinner. Winter was coming and Sag Harbor was bleak and cold. All the egrets were gone, and there were only swans and geese on the ponds—sitting like statues on the frozen waters. Arnold and I went around feeding them with bags of bread. And then we would go back to the dog grooming parlor and make love. Limited, limited love.

Let's get engaged, I would say. Please Arnold, just give me a ring or something. Not until you are eighteen, he would reply, people your age can change. I would sit up on the couch and look at him, my clothes disheveled, my heart pounding, and declare, This can't go on much longer, Arnold, I'm near the breaking point. Be patient, he would reply, things will work out.

I will love you for the rest of my life! I would say. *Please.* Let's get engaged.

What people feel at sixteen, they do not always feel at thirty, Arnold replied. Youth is changeable.

Was it because he was from Kansas? Because he had been raised in the Presbyterian church? Because his parents were solemn and strict? Was it because he loved me, or didn't love me enough? I could not figure out the reason for Arnold's reticence, but it drove me wild, and one night I even tried to get him drunk so I could seduce him. But Arnold, I learned, did not get drunk— the reason being that he drank like Queen Victoria. Tiny sips. It took him one whole evening to finish a scotch and soda.

I think you will agree with me that it is a peculiar thing when a woman wants to lose her virginity and the man won't cooperate. And, to make the whole thing worse, a postcard from Nicole had arrived from Paris, where she and Robert were honeymooning. "Darling Mouse," the postcard said, "we think of you and Arnold with affection. Robert, he still make love most beautifully. I am not bored."

23

THEN IT WAS CHRISTMASTIME, and all the trees on Main Street were lit with little white lights. The windmill near the harbor was lit up too, and all the stores looked festive. In the window of the Craft Gallery an old toy train went round and round, teddy bears sitting in the boxcars. At the Shell Shop across the street, poinsettia plants bloomed amid the seashells. Everywhere you looked there was light and color to offset the gloomy weather—and Arnold and I were more in love than ever.

We had acquired another kitten—which made three—and had bought a small television set. We had gone to a thrift shop and found a faded but beautiful rug for the living room. We had purchased new lamps and cooking pots, and had installed a kerosene heater in Arnold's bedroom, which was always cold. But we were not yet lovers.

What I intended to give Arnold for Christmas was *me*—all of me—but I did not know how to do it. Emerge from the shower one evening wearing nothing but a red ribbon? Dress up like a girl Santa and seduce him? No, these were vulgar thoughts, and the one thing Arnold Bromberg was not, was vulgar.

And then it hit me. We would get married.

Forget the engagement, I thought, and forget the diamond ring. Forget the parties and celebrations. Arnold Bromberg and I are going to get married, even if I have to hypnotize him. Even if he's unaware of the whole event.

It happened on Christmas Eve. School had been out for a week, and Arnold and I had been busy shopping, buying presents for his parents, and my parents, and everyone else we knew. We bought presents for the kittens—Wynken, Blynken, and Nod—and for Daisy the goat. We even bought a small present for Robert and Nicole and mailed it to Paris.

That evening, Christmas Eve, Arnold and I had dinner with my parents, and then we went back to the dog grooming parlor. Our plan was to decorate the huge tree we had bought and placed in the living room, and go to midnight services at the Whalers Church. But I had something else in mind. "Arnold?" I said, as we began to put the Christmas lights on the tree. "Arnold dear?"

"Yes, sweetie?" He was busy untangling a rope of blue lights, and was not paying much attention to me. Fascinated by the lights, the three kittens sat on the floor watching, ready to pounce.

"Would you come to church with me tonight a little early? So we could sit there and just enjoy the atmosphere?"

"What atmosphere?" Arnold said vaguely. He was still working on the tangled lights.

"You know. The church and the decorations and everything. You could even play me some organ music."

He smiled tolerantly and stretched the rope of blue lights out on the floor. All three kittens pounced. "Do you want a rope of blue, and then one of red?" he asked. "Or should it be the other way around?"

I went over and kissed him. "I love you," I said. "It's Christmas and I love you."

We embraced as the kittens batted the rope of lights he had laid out on the floor. A powdery snow was falling outside, and far in the distance some children were caroling. "Silent night," they sang, "holy night. All is calm, all is bright."

We were still holding each other close. "So will you?" I asked.

Arnold kissed the top of my head. "Will I what, dearest?"

"Come to church with me early?"

"Yes," he said. "Of course."

By ten o'clock the snow was pouring down on Sag Harbor, thick, fine, powdery snow. Arnold and I wrapped ourselves up in scarves and caps and winter coats. In boots and mittens. Then we set out for the church. There were trees lit everywhere, on people's lawns and in people's living rooms. On back porches, in backyards, and even in the middle of the town pond—a tiny Christmas tree on a raft, lit with white lights.

"The church may not be open yet," Arnold said, as we approached Union Street. "It's only ten o'clock."

But it was open, and after brushing the snow from our boots, we went inside. I caught my breath—because the Whalers Church looked so beautiful. The stark pale-green interior was decorated with poinsettia plants, and the altar was a bower of green leaves and red berries. It was empty and quiet, with no one around and my heart was beating very quickly because of my plan.

We sat down in a pew, and Arnold lowered his head and said a silent prayer. I did the same, saying, "God, I'm not an atheist anymore, so I hope you're listening. Please help me tonight. Thank you."

"Will you play some music for me?" I said to Arnold. "Nobody's here, and even if they were, I don't think they'd mind."

He nodded, and—just like the first time we had been in this church—he disappeared and mounted the creaky back stairway. In a second he appeared on the balcony and waved at me. He sat down at the organ.

Don't ask me how I knew this, but I just knew that he would play the "Dorian Toccata" by Bach—the one I had admired last summer. And he did. Within a moment the music was filling the church with a huge golden sound.

Arnold played for around fifteen minutes. Beautifully, brilliantly. Then he came down the stairs again and into the church.

He did not find me where he had left me, because I was standing on the altar, looking out at the empty church. "Dearly beloved," I said.

Dearly beloved, we are gathering here tonight to join this man and this woman in holy matrimony. His name is Arnold and her name is Rita, and they love each other. They're not ready to get married yet, but they do love each other, so this ceremony will have to do for the moment.

"Come here," I said to Arnold. "We're getting married."

The look on his face was so marvelous that I almost laughed. But since this was my wedding, I did not wish to spoil it with levity. "Arnold Bromberg," I said. "Come here."

Looking astonished, Arnold came up to the altar and stood by my side. I had bought two wedding bands at the dime store. Not real gold, but what the hell. They were our rings and they were going to join us in the bonds of matrimony. "Take my hand," I said to Arnold, and he did.

"Do you, Arnold Bromberg, marry me, Rita Formica?" I asked. "Do you accept this temporary arrangement until I am eighteen?"

"Yes," he said softly. "I do."

I slipped one of the rings on Arnold's wedding finger. "Good. Because I, Rita Formica, marry you too. I marry you because I love you and will never love anyone else. Amen."

I handed the second ring to Arnold, and he slipped it on my finger. We looked at each other for a long long time. At last our lips met, and it was the dearest, sweetest kiss we had ever given each other. A kiss like heaven.

24

ON CHRISTMAS MORNING I woke in Arnold Bromberg's bed, in Arnold Bromberg's arms. Snow was falling, and the three kittens were asleep at our feet. Far away, a church bell was tolling. In the bird feeder outside the window, a bright-red cardinal sang.

I had lost my virginity—as the saying goes—but the funny thing is that nothing had been lost at all. Instead, something had been found, something incredible that I had only read about in books. Call it passion if you will, but it was deeper than that. Too deep for words.

I looked at Arnold, at his sleeping face and curly hair, at his naked shoulders, and at his large hands folded on the blanket. I looked at him and saw my present and my past—and also my future. I saw myself thin and I saw myself grown up. I saw us married for the rest of our lives.

"Arnold?" I said, shaking him gently. "Arnold dear?"

"Umm?" he muttered in his sleep. "Yes?"

"Could you wake up for a minute?"

He smiled vaguely. "I don't think so. Is it . . . anything important?"

"It's nothing," I whispered, kissing his ear. "Go back to sleep, my darling. I just wanted to tell you that you were right about something. The universe *is* benevolent."